It was such a sma... ...as-
ily covered it, and ... ...the gun and her hand
together in a viselike grip, smiling as if he were just
greeting an old acquaintance, until the wail of the
sirens died away.

"Do you really want to go to a police station?"
he drawled. "I'm not so fond of them myself, and
usually they aren't very fond of me. Wouldn't you
rather have a drink?"

Thus the Saint once again charms his way
through these exciting adventures:

Don't miss other Ace Charter titles in the Saint series:

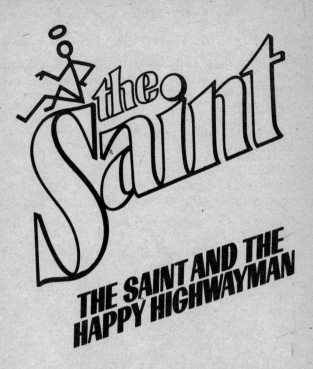

THE SAINT AND THE HAPPY HIGHWAYMAN

LESLIE CHARTERIS

CHARTER
NEW YORK

A Division of Charter Communications Inc.
A GROSSET & DUNLAP COMPANY
51 Madison Avenue
New York, New York 10010

THE HAPPY HIGHWAYMAN

An Ace Charter Book
by arrangement with Doubleday and Company, Inc.

First Ace Charter Printing: July, 1981
Published simultaneously in Canada

2 4 6 8 0 9 7 5 3 1
Manufactured in the United States of America

I THE MAN WHO WAS LUCKY

"THE REBEL OF YESTERDAY is the hero of tomorrow. Simon Templar, known as The Saint, whose arrest was the ambition of every policeman in the city two years ago on account of his extralegal activities against the gangs of the bootleg era, comes back to New York on a pleasure trip with the tacit consent of the Police Department.

"The converse is also true.

"Lucky Joe Luckner, last surviving great name of the racketeers of the same period, once the friend of judges and the privileged pet of politicians, stands his trial for income-tax evasions with a life term on Alcatraz Island in prospect.

"We see no need for Simon Templar to go back to his old games. The crooks are being taken care of as they should be, by the men who are employed to do so, with the whole force of an aroused public opinion behind them."

Thus somewhat optimistically spoke the editorial writer of the New York *Daily Mail*, on a certain morning in the beginning of the spring.

Simon Templar kept the cutting. He had a weakness for collecting the miscellaneous items of publicity with which the press punctuated his career from time to time. He had been publicly called a great many names in his life and they all interested him. To those who found themselves sadder or poorer or even deader by reason of his interference in their nefarious activities, he was an unprintable illegitimate; to those whose melancholy duty it was to discourage his blithe propensity for taking the law into his own hands, he was a perpetually disturbing problem; to a few people he was a hero; to himself he was only an adventurer, finding the best romance he could in a dull mechanical age, fighting crime because he had to fight something, and not caring too much whether he himself transgressed the law in doing so. Sometimes his adventures left him poorer, more often they left him richer; but always they were exciting. Which was all that the Saint asked of life.

He showed the cutting to Inspector John Fernack down on Centre Street a few days after his arrival, and the detective rubbed his square pugnacious chin.

"There's somethin' in it," he said.

Simon detected the faintly hesitant inflection in the other's voice and raised his eyebrows gently.

"Why only something?"

"You've seen the papers?"

The Saint shrugged.

"Well, he hasn't been acquitted."

"No, he hasn't been acquitted." The detective's tone was blunt and sardonic. "Lucky Joe's luck didn't hold that far. But what the hell? The next jury that takes the case can't help rememberin' that the first jury disagreed, and that means it'll be twice as hard to make 'em find him guilty. And nobody cares so much about a second trial. I don't say we won't get him eventually—the Feds might

have got him this time if one of the witnesses
hadn't been taken for a ride and a couple of others
hadn't disappeared. But look what they're trying'
to get him for. Income tax!"

"It's been used before."

"Income tax!" Fernack took the words in his
teeth and worried it like a dog. The smouldering
heat of his indignation came up into his eyes.
"What d'ya think that means? All it means is that
everybody else who ought to of put Luckner away
has fallen down. All it means is that so many
crooked politicians and crook lawyers an' crook
police chiefs have been playing ball with him so
long that now there ain't any other charge left to
bring against him. All it means is that for fifteen
years this guy Luckner has been a racketeer and a
murderer, and now the only rap they can stick on
him is that he never paid any income tax!"

The Saint nodded thoughtfully.

"You know all these things about him are true?"

"Listen," said Fernack with fierce and caustic
restraint. "When a guy who tried to muscle in on
Luckner's territory was found dead in a ditch in the
Bronx, you bet Luckner didn't have nothin' to do
with it. When a cop tried to stop one of Luckner's
beer trucks back in prohibition days and got shot
in the belly, you bet Luckner was sorry for him.
Yeah, Luckner would always be sorry for a fool
cop who butted in when the guys higher up said to
lay off. When half-a-dozen poolroom keepers got
beaten up because they don't join Luckner's
poolroom union, you bet Luckner cried when he
heard about it. And when one of the witnesses
against him in this trial gets bumped off and two
others fade away into thin air, you take your shirt
off and bet everything you've got it just makes

Lucky Joe's heart bleed to think about it." Fernack took the cigar out of his mouth and spat explosively. "You know your way around as well as I do, Saint, or you used to. And you ask me that!"

Simon swung a long leg over the arm of his chair and gazed at the detective through the drifting smoke of his cigarette with a glimpse of idle mockery twinkling deep down in his blue eyes.

"One gathers that Lucky Joe wouldn't be so lucky if you got him alone in a back alley on a dark night," he remarked.

"Say, listen." Fernack's huge hands rested on the top of his desk, solid as battering rams, looking as if they could have crashed clean through the fragile timber if he had thumped it to emphasize his point. "If they put Luckner in the chair six days runnin' and fried him six times he wouldn't get more than the law's been owin' him for the last ten years. That guy's a rat an' a killer—a natural born louse from the day he was weaned—"

He stopped rather abruptly, as though he had only just realised the trend of his argument. Perhaps the quietly speculative smile on the Saint's lips, and the rakish lines of the dark fighting face, brought back too many memories to let him continue with an easy conscience. For there had been days, before that tacit amnesty to which the editorial writer of the New York *Daily Mail* had referred, when that lean debonair outlaw lounging in his armchair had led the New York police a dance that would be remembered in their annals for many years—when the elusive figure of the Saint had first loomed up on the dark horizons of the city's underworld and taken the law into his own hands to such effect that fully half-a-dozen once famous names could be found carved on tombstones in certain cemeteries to mark the tempestuousness of his passing.

"I don't mean what you're thinkin'," Fernack said heavily. "Luckner is goin' to be taken care of. Even if he only gets a life term on Alcatraz it'll be somethin'. I know you did a few things for us a coupla years back that we couldn't do ourselves on account of the way all the politicians were holding onto us. But that's all changed now. We got a different setup. Luckner isn't goin' to the chair now because the politicians of a couple years back let him loose; but anybody who tries to pull any of that stuff now isn't goin' to find it so easy to get away with. That goes for you too. Just stick around and have a good time, and you won't be interfered with. Go back to your old line, and you and me will be fightin' again. With this difference—that you won't have the excuse that you had the last time."

The Saint grinned lazily.

"Okay," he murmured, "I'll remember it."

His tone was so innocent and docile that Fernack glared at him for a moment suspiciously; but the Saint laughed at him and took him out to lunch and talked to him so engagingly about the most harmless topics that that momentary flash of uneasiness had faded from the detective's mind by the time they parted. Which was exactly what the Saint meant it to do. The Saint never asked for superfluous trouble—quite enough of it came his way in the normal course of events without encouraging him to invite extra donations without good reason.

As a matter of fact, the luck of Lucky Joe Luckner might well have slipped away into the background of his memory and remained there permanently. He had really come back to America for a holiday, with no thoughts of crime in his head. For a few days, at least, the bright lights of Broadway would provide all the excitement he needed; and after that he would move on somewhere else.

He had thought no more about it a couple of days later when he saw a face that he remembered coming out of a travel agency on Fifth Avenue. The girl was so intent on hurrying through the crowd that she might not have noticed him, but he caught her arm as she went by and turned her around.

"Hello, Cora," he drawled.

She looked at him with a queer mixture of fear and defiance that surprised him. The look had vanished a moment after she recognised him, but it remained in his memory with the beginning of a question mark after it. He kept his hand on her arm.

"Why—hello, Saint!"

He smiled.

"Hush," he said. "Not so loud. I may be an honest citizen to all intents and purposes, but I haven't got used to it. Come and have a drink and tell me the story of your life."

"I'm sorry." Did he imagine that she still seemed a trifle breathless, just as he might have imagined that swift glimmer of fright in her eyes when he caught hold of her? "Not just now. Can't we have lunch or something tomorrow? I—I've got an appointment."

"With Marty?"

He was sure now. There was a perceptible hesitation before she answered, exactly as if she had paused to consider whether she should tell him the truth or invent a story.

"Yes. Please—I'm in a hurry . . ."

"So am I." The Saint's voice was innocently persuasive. "Can I give you a lift? I'd like to see Marty again."

"I'm afraid he's ill."

This was a lie. The Saint knew it, but the genial persuasion of his smile didn't alter. Those who knew him best had learned that that peculiarly lazy and aimless smile was the index of a crystallising determination which was harder to resist than most other men's square-jawed aggression.

A taxi stood conveniently empty by the curb. He opened the door; and he still held her arm.

"Where to?" he asked as they settled down.

She leaned her head back and closed her eyes. After a moment she gave him an address. He relayed it to the driver and took out a packet of cigarettes. They rode on for a while in silence, and he studied her thoughtfully without seeming to stare. She had always been pretty in a fair-haired and rather fluffy way, but now for the first time he was aware of a background of character which he hadn't noticed particularly when he had known her before. Perhaps it had always been there, but he hadn't observed her closely enough to see it.

He cast his mind back over the time when they had first met. She was going around with Marty O'Connor then, and apparently they were still going around. That indicated some kind of character at least—he wasn't quite sure what kind. After they had driven a few blocks he reached forward and closed the glass partition to shut them off from the driver.

"Well, dear heart, do you tell me about it or do I drag it out of you? Is Marty in trouble again?"

She nodded hesitantly.

The Saint drew at his cigarette without any visible indications of surprise. When one is a minor racketeer, strong-arm man and reputed gunman like Marty O'Connor, one is liable to be in trouble pretty frequently. Simon concentrated for a moment on trying to blow a couple of smoke rings. The draft from the open window broke them up, and he said: "Who started it?"

"Why do you want to know?"

"Marty did something for me once. If he's in trouble I'd like to do something for him. I suppose it's immoral, but I always had a soft spot for that old thug. On the level, Cora."

"You're not tied up with the cops any more?"

"I never was. I just did some of their work for them once, but they never thanked me. And if I'd ever had anything to take out on Marty I'd have done it years ago."

She looked at him for some seconds before she answered, and then her answer was only made indirectly. She leaned forward and opened the partition again just long enough to change the address he had given the driver to another two blocks north of it.

"You know the game," said the Saint appreciatively, and for the first time she looked him full in the eyes.

"I have to," she said. "The G-men have been combing the town for Marty for the last three months."

Simon raised his eyebrows without emotion.

"What did he do? Did he take up kidnapping, or is he another of these income-tax defaulters?"

She looked at him queerly for a moment, and when she laughed there was a sharp note of strain in the sound.

"The trouble is he knows too much about income tax. He'd be the star witness against Luckner if they could get his evidence."

"And he doesn't want to give it?"

"He doesn't want to die," said the girl brutally.

Simon put his feet up on the spare seat opposite him and smoked placidly. Coincidence was a queer thing, but he had ceased to marvel at its complexities. Once again, through that chance encounter, he found the subject of Lucky Joe Luckner thrust into his mind, and the repetition gave it enough weight to make it stay there. But he was wise enough not to press the girl for any more details during the drive. In due course of time he would know all that he wanted to know; and he was prepared to wait. He would see Marty himself.

The cab stopped outside a dingy brick house between Ninth and Tenth avenues. A half-dozen grimy gutter-snipes were playing raucous baseball in the street. The windows in the front of the house were clouded with the accumulated dirt of ages. Inside the front door, the dark hall was paved with a strip of threadbare linoleum, and Simon felt the slithery gloss of thick dust under his finger tips when he put his hand on the banister as they climbed the stairs to the second floor. His nose wrinkled in response to a faint pervasive odour of ancient cooking. And a slight frown creased itself into his forehead. He was still a long way from having all his questions answered. To find Marty O'Connor in a place like this, even as a hideout, was a mystery in itself—Marty who had always been such a swell dresser with a highly developed taste for spring mattresses and Turkey carpets and flashy decoration.

The girl opened the door and they went into the

living room. The furniture there was in keeping with what anyone would have expected from a preliminary glance of the building—cheap, shoddy and shabby—but Simon noticed that unlike the rest of the place it appeared to be clean. Cora pulled off her hat.

"Hello, Marty," she called. "I brought a friend to see you."

Marty O'Connor appeared in the doorway of the bedroom. He was in his shirt sleeves, a shirt open at the neck, and he kept one hand in his pocket. He stared at the Saint blankly, and then his homely face broke into a slow gold-and-ivory grin.

"Well for . . . Where the hell did you come from?"

The Saint chuckled. Marty took his right hand out of his pocket for the first time and Simon grasped it.

"I wouldn't have believed you could get any uglier, Marty, but you made it."

The gunman hauled him towards a chair and sat him down. He looked a little less plump than he had been when the Saint saw him last, and there seemed to be a trace of hollowness in his unshaven cheeks; but the feckless twinkles in his faded eyes was the same as that by which Simon had first been beguiled from his antipathy for the ordinary run of hoodlums.

"I sure am glad to see you here again, Saint. It's a long time since we had a drink together." O'Connor dusted the table with his handkerchief and sat on it. He turned round. "Cora! See if you got any of that gin left we had the other night . . . Say!" He looked at the Saint again, beaming with a simple pleasure that had temporarily wiped away the furtive defensiveness with which he had emerged from the bedroom. "Where you been all this time?"

"Here and there," said the Saint vaguely. "I've covered a good deal of ground. Have you been looking after yourself?"

"Not so badly."

The girl came back into the room, bearing a garrishly labelled bottle, and three cheap glasses.

"It's okay, Marty," she said. "I told him."

The gunman scratched his head. For a moment his heavy face sank back into its mask of dour suspicion. And then he grinned rather ruefully, like an unrepentant urchin.

"Well, ya know how it is, Saint," he said apologetically.

Simon shook his head.

"That's just what I don't quite know."

Marty tipped liquor into the three glasses and passed one of them over. He sat down again.

"Well . . ." He picked a half-smoked cigarette out of the ash tray and relighted it. "All the good business folded after repeal. Sure, you could always give somebody a bit of protection, but you couldn't get the same dough. Besides, Luckner couldn't keep the connections he used to have since the city got a new administration. Some of the mob took up kidnapping but that ain't my idea of a man's job. It got too dangerous at that. I just about decided the best thing was to go on the legit if I could find a job anywhere—and then this Luckner case blew up. Didya read about it in the papers?"

"I've heard of it."

"I useta work with Luckner once—you know when. I never liked him, but it was just business. You know we nearly had a fight lotsa times when he was tryin' to make Cora go out with him."

"He never did any harm," said the girl lightly.

"And that wasn't for want of tryin'," growled O'Connor. "Why, I never see a guy make such a play for a girl like he done for Cora. Why, he once told her he'd have me taken for a ride and marry her himself if she'd say the word." Marty laughed in his throat, but the sound was without humour. "You only can trust that guy as far as you can trust a rattlesnake. Still, I wouldn't stop him findin' his own way outta this income-tax rap if he can do it. I hear the G-men wanted me for a witness—I useta keep his accounts once—so I pulled out and went underground. I know things that wouldn't've let him get away with a hung jury last time. But what's that worth?"

"It might have been worth a fresh start to you, Marty," said the Saint speculatively.

The other grinned slowly.

"Yeah, a fresh start under a slab of marble. I wouldn't lift a finger for Lucky if he was gonna burn tomorrer. But hell, I ain't a squealer. Besides, you know what happened to Snaky Romaro and those other two guys what were going to give evidence?" Marty's big mouth turned down at the corners with cynical significance. "I ain't no Little Lord Fauntleroy, but I know Lucky, and I know his gang has orders what to do about any guy that turns up as a witness against him. So, Cora and me we come here where we figger nobody will ever look for us, and we stay here ever since. It ain't been easy, with no dough comin' in—but we're still alive."

The Saint's blue eyes travelled slowly over the apartment again; took in the dingy carpet worn down almost to its backing, the wobble of the rickety table on which Marty had perched, the hideous upholstery of the gimcrack chairs.

"I suppose it would be difficult," he said.

Marty nodded.

"We had our bit of luck," he said. "I got a job the other day. Just wonderin' what we were gonna do next. I remembered a pal of mine who went to Canada two-three years back and got himself a garage. He ain't got so much money either, but he wrote back he could give me a job startin' at twenny bucks a week if I could find my way up there. Cora went around and borrowed some dough—she had to be pretty careful 'cause they're lookin' for her too, knowin' she'd probably lead 'em back to me. She went out an' bought our tickets today—I guess that's when you must of met her. So if I can get clear without bein' stopped we oughta get along all right."

Simon didn't laugh, although for a moment the idea of Marty O'Connor, who had seen the big money and flashed it around as liberally as anyone else in his class, washing cars for twenty dollars a week was humorous enough. But he looked round the apartment again and his gaze came to rest on the face of the girl Cora with a certain understanding. He knew now what subconscious intuition had made him revise his casual opinion of her, even in those brief minutes in the taxi. Stranger things have happened in that unpredictable sub-stratum of civilisation with which he had spent half his life.

"It's a pity you can't take some dough with you and buy a share in this garage business," he said; and knew before he started to elaborate the suggestion into an offer that it would be refused.

Later on in the evening he had an even better idea, and he talked for half an hour before he was able to induce Marty to accept it. What argument it was that finally turned the scale he would have found it hard to remember. But once the Saint was on the trail of an inspiration he had a gift of persuasiveness that would have sold a line of rubber boots to a colony of boa constrictors.

Lucky Joe Luckner, recuperating from the ordeal of his trial in his hotel suite at Briarcliff, was still satisfied with his consistent good luck in spite of the two quiet and inconspicuous men who sat around in the hotel lobby all day and followed him at a discreet distance whenever he went out. He had no intention of jumping his bail. The drastic entry of the Department of Justice into the war with crime had made the role of a fugitive from justice even less attractive than it had been before. Luckner had never been a fugitive—he couldn't imagine himself in the part. Quite confidently, he was waiting for an acquittal in his next trial which would leave him a free man without a single legal stain on his character; and if his attorney did not quite share this sublime confidence, he had to admit that the result of the first trial lent some support to it.

"Betcha they can't box me in twenty years," he declared boastfully, to his personal bodyguard.

The saturnine Mr. Toscelli agreed encouragingly, which was one of his lighter duties, and Lucky Joe rewarded him with a slap on the back and a cigar. Few men are offended by hearing their boasts enthusiastically echoed, and Luckner was known to be rather more than ordinarily vulnerable.

He was a short, thickset man who looked rather more like a truck driver than a beer baron, with small close-set eyes and a big coarse laugh. His extravagances were of a type that ran to loud check suits, yellow spats, strangely hued hats and large diamonds; and he imagined that these outward evidences of good taste and prosperity were part of the secret of his hypnotic power over women. This hypnotic power was one of his more whimsical fantasies, but his associates had found it healthier to accept it with tactful solemnity. He boasted that he had never failed to conquer any woman whom he had desired to possess, and he had a convenient faculty for forgetting the many exceptions which tended to disprove the rule. But apart from this one playful weakness he was as sentimental as a scorpion; and the Saint estimated the probabilities with some care before he approached Lucky Joe in person.

If he had been cautious he would never have gone at all, but Simon Templar was a confirmed believer in direct action, and he knew exactly the strength of his hand.

He drove out to Briarcliff on a pleasant sunny day and sauntered up the steps under the critical eyes of a dozen disapproving residents who were sunning themselves on the terrace. The Saint could see no good reason why they should be disapproving, for he felt very contented with himself that morning and considered that he was more than ordinarily beautiful and definitely an ornament to the scenery; but he realised that the knowledge that Lucky Joe Luckner was a fellow guest must have cast a certain amount of cloud over the tranquillity of the other inmates of that highly respectable hostelry, and made his own excuses for their lack of visible appreciation. Perhaps they had some good reason to fear that a man with that loose and rather buccaneering stride and that rather reckless

cut of face was only another manifestation of the
underworld invasion which had disturbed the
peace of their rural retreat, and in a way they were
right; but the Saint didn't care. With his hands in
his pockets and his spotless white Panama tilted
jauntily over one eye, he wandered on into the
lounge and identified two blue-chinned individ-
uals, who lifted flat fishlike eyes from their newspapers at his advent, as being more deserving of the
reception committee's disapproving stares than
himself. There were also two large men with heavy
shoulders and big feet sitting in another corner of
the lounge, who inspected him with a similar air of
inquiry; but neither party knew him, and he went
up the stairs unquestioned.

The door of Luckner's suite opened at his knock
to exhibit another blue chin and flat fishlike stare
similar to those which had greeted him downstairs.
It stayed open just far enough for that, and the
stare absorbed him with the expressionlessness of a
dead cod.

"Hullo, body," murmured the Saint easily.
"When did they dig you up?"

The stare darkened, without taking on any more
expression.

"Whaddaya want?" it asked flatly.

"I want to see Lucky Joe."

"He ain't here."

"Tell him it's about Marty O'Connor," said the
Saint gently. "And tell him he doesn't know how
lucky he is."

The man looked at him for a moment longer and
then closed the door suddenly. Simon lighted a
cigarette and waited patiently. The door opened
again.

"Come in."

Simon went in. The man who had let him in stayed behind him, with his back to the door. Another man of similarly taciturn habits and lack of facial expression sat on the arm of a chair by the window, with one hand in his coat pocket, thoughtfully picking his teeth with the other. Luckner sat on the settee, in his shirt sleeves, with his feet on a low table. He took the cigar out of his mouth and looked at the Saint reflectively.

Simon came to a halt in front of him and touched two fingers to the brim of his hat in a lazy and ironical salute. He smiled, with a faint twinkle in his blue eyes, and Luckner glowered at him uncertainly.

"Well—what is it?"

The Saint put his cigarette to his lips.

"I just dropped in," he said. "I wondered if you looked quite as nasty in the flesh as the stories I've read about you made you out to be. Also because I heard you'd be interested in any news about Marty O'Connor."

"Where is he?"

Simon's smile widened by a vague seraphic fraction.

"That's my secret."

Luckner took his feet off the table and got up slowly until he faced the Saint. He was six inches shorter than Simon but he thrust his lumpy red face up as close as he could under the Saint's nose.

"Where is he?"

"It's just possible," said the Saint in his slow soft voice, without a shift of his eyes, "that you've got some mistaken ideas about what I am and what I've come here for. If you had an idea, for instance, that your ugly mug was so terrifying that I'd fold up as soon as I saw it, or that I'd tell you anything

until I was ready to tell it—well, we'd better go
back to the beginning and start again."

Luckner glared at him silently for a second, and
then he said in a very level tone: "Who the hell are
you?"

"I am the Saint."

The man on the arm of the chair took the toothpick out of his mouth and forgot to close his mouth
behind it. The man by the door sucked in his
breath with a sharp hiss like a squirt of escaping
steam. Only Luckner made no active expression of
emotion, but his face went a shade lighter in color
and froze into wooden restraint.

Simon allowed the announcement to sink into
the brains of his audience at its own good leisure,
while he let the smoke of his cigarette trickle
through his lips to curl in a faintly mocking feather
before Luckner's stony eyes. There was something
so serene, something so strong and quietly dangerous about him which coupled with his almost
apologetic self-introduction was like the revelation
of an unsheathed sword, that none of the men
made any move towards him. He looked at
Luckner unruffledly with those very clear and
faintly bantering blue eyes.

"I am the Saint," he said. "You should know the
name. I know where to find Marty O'Connor. The
only question you have to answer is—how much is
he worth to you?"

Luckner's knees bent until he reached the level
of the settee. He put the cigar back in his mouth.

"Sit down," he said. "Let's talk this over."

The Saint shook his head.

"Why spend the time, Joe? You ought to know
how much Marty's worth. I hear he used to keep
your accounts once, and he could make a great

squeal if they got him on the stand. It'd put three new lives into the prosecution. Not that I'd lose any sleep if they were going to send you to the chair; but I suppose we can't put everything right at once. You'll get what's coming to you. Sooner or later. But just for the moment, this is more important." Simon studied his fingernails. "I owe Marty something, but I can't give it to him myself —that's one of the disadvantages of the wave of virtue which seems to have come over this great country. But I don't see why you shouldn't give him what he deserves." The Saint's eyes lifted again suddenly to Luckner's face with a cold and laconic directness. "I don't care what you do about Marty so long as I get what I think he's worth."

"And what's that?"

"That is just one hundred grand."

Luckner stiffened as if a spear had been rammed up his backbone from his sacrum to his scalp.

"How much?"

"One hundred thousand dollars," said the Saint calmly. "And cheap at the price. After all, that's less than a third of what you offered the Revenue to get this income-tax case dropped altogether. . . . You will pay it in twenty-dollar bills, and I shall want it by ten o'clock tonight."

The dilated incredulity of Luckner's eyes remained set for a moment, and then they narrowed back to their normal size and remained fixed on the Saint's face like glittering beads. It was symptomatic of Luckner's psychology that he made no further attempt to argue. The Saint didn't have the air of a man who was prepared to devote any time to bargaining, and Luckner knew it. It didn't even occur to him to question the fundamental fact of whether Simon Templar was really in a position to carry out his share of the transaction. The Saint's name, and the reputation which Luckner still remembered, was a sufficient guarantee of that. There was only one flimsy quibble that Luckner could see at all, and he had a premonition that even this was hopeless before he tried it.

"Suppose we kept you here without any hundred grand and just saw what we could do about persuading you to tell us where Marty is?"

"Of course I'd never have thought of that. It wouldn't have occurred to me to have somebody waiting outside here who'd start back for New York if I didn't come out of this room safe and sound in"—he looked at his watch—"just under another three minutes. And I wouldn't have thought of telling this guy that if he had to beat it back to the city without me he was to get Marty and take him straight along to the D.A.'s office. . . . You're taking an awful lot for granted, Joe, but if you think you can make me talk in two and a half minutes go ahead and try."

Luckner chewed his cigar deliberately across from one side of his mouth to the other. He was in a corner, and he was capable of facing the fact.

"Where do we make the trade?"

"You can send a couple of guys with the money down the Bronx River Parkway tonight. I'll be waiting in a car one mile south of a sign on the right which says City of Yonkers. If the dough is okay I'll tell them where to find Marty, and they can have him in five minutes. What they do when they see him is none of my business." The Saint's blue eyes rested on Luckner again with the same quiet and deadly implication. "Is that all quite clear?"

Luckner's head remained poised for a moment

before it jerked briefly downwards.

"The dough will be okay," he said, and the Saint smiled again.

"They didn't know how lucky you were going to be when they gave you your nickname, Joe," he said.

For some time after he had gone, Luckner sat in the same position, with his hands on his spread knees, chewing his cigar and staring impassively in front of him. The man with the toothpick continued his endless foraging. The man who had guarded the door lighted a cigarette and gazed vacantly out of the window.

The situation was perfectly clear, and Luckner had enough cold-blooded detachment to review it with his eyes open. After a while he spoke.

"You better go, Luigi," he said. "You and Karlatta. Take a coupla typewriters, and don't waste any time."

Toscelli nodded phlegmatically and garaged his toothpick in his vest pocket.

"Do we take the dough?"

"You're damn right you take the dough. You heard what he said? You give him the dough an' he tells you where to find Marty. I'll write some checks and you can go to New York this afternoon and collect it. An' don't kid yourselves. If there are any tricks, that son of a bitch has thought of them all. You know how he took off Morrie Ualino an' Dutch Kuhlmann?"

"It's a lot of dough, Lucky," said Mr. Toscelli gloomily.

Joe Luckner's jaw hardened.

"A life on Alcatraz is a lot of years," he said stolidly. "Never mind the dough. Just see that Marty keeps his mouth shut. Maybe we can do something about the dough afterwards.''

Even then he kept his belief in his lucky star, although the benefit it had conferred on him was somewhat ambiguous. A more captious man might have quibbled that a price ticket of one hundred thousand dollars was an expensive present, but to Luckner it represented fair value. Nor did he feel any compunction about the use to which he proposed to put the gift.

In this respect, at least, Toscelli was able to agree with him without placing any strain on his principles. The chief load on his mind was the responsibility of the cargo of twenty-dollar bills which he had collected from various places during the afternoon; and he felt a certain amount of relief when he arrived at the rendezvous and found a closed car parked by the roadside and waiting for him exactly as the Saint had promised that it would be. Even so, he kept one hand on his gun while the Saint received the heavy packages of currency through the window.

Simon examined each packet carefully under the dashboard light and satisfied himself that there was no deception.

"A very nice little haul," he murmured. "You must be sorry to see it go, Luigi. . . . By the way, you can let go your gun—I've got you covered from here, and you're a much better target than I am."

Toscelli wavered, peering at him somberly out of the gloom. It was true that it grieved him to see so much hard cash taken out of his hands; but he remembered Luckner's warning, and he had heard of the Saint's reputation himself.

"Where do we go?" he growled.

The shiny barrel of the Saint's automatic, resting

on the edge of the window, moved in a briefly indicative arc towards the north.

"Straight on up the Parkway for exactly three miles. Park your wagon there and wait for results. He'll be travelling south, looking for a car parked exactly where you're going to be—but he won't expect you to be in it. You won't make any mistake, because I've marked his car: the near-side headlight has a cross of adhesive tape on the lens, and I hope it will give you pious ideas. On your way, brother. . . ."

Simon drove slowly south. In about half a mile he pulled in to the side of the road again and stopped there. He flicked his headlights two or three times before he finally switched them out, and he was completing the task of distributing a measured half of Toscelli's hundred-thousand-dollar payment over his various pockets when a subdued voice hailed him cautiously from the shadows at the roadside.

The Saint grinned and opened the door.

"Hullo there, Marty." He settled his pockets, buttoned his coat and slipped out. "Are you ready to travel?"

"If there's nothing to stop us."

"There isn't." Simon punched him gently in the stomach and their hands met. "The car is yours, and you'll find about fifty thousand bucks lying about in it. The earth is yours between here and the Canadian border; but if I were you I'd strike east from here and go up through White Plains. And any time I'm in Canada I'll drop by your garage for some gas. Maybe it'll go towards evening up what you did for me one time." He gripped Marty's shoulder for a moment and then turned to the other slighter figure which stood beside them. "Take care of him, Cora—and yourself too."

"I'll do that."

A match flared in the Saint's hands for an instant, but his eyes were intent on the cigarette he was lighting.

"You called Lucky Joe as I told you to?" he asked casually, "Told him you were through with Marty and couldn't bear to wait another day to take up with the new love?"

"Yes. Half an hour ago."

"I bet he fell for it."

"He said he'd be there." She hesitated. "I don't know why you've done all this for us, Saint, and I don't know how you did it—but why did you want me to do that?"

The Saint smiled invisibly in the dark.

"Because I made an appointment for him and I wanted to be sure he'd keep it. Some friends of his will be there to meet him. I have to work in these devious ways these days because Inspector Fernack warned me to keep out of trouble. Don't lose any sleep over it, kid. Be good."

He kissed her, and held the door while they got into the car. From somewhere far to the north the faint rattle of machine guns came down the wind.

II   THE SMART DETECTIVE

LIEUTENANT CORRIO was on the carpet. This was a unique experience for him, for he had a rather distinguished record on the New York Detective Bureau. Since the time when he was admitted to it, he had achieved a series of successes which had earned him more than ordinarily rapid promotion without winning him any of the affection of his colleagues and superiors. While he had made comparatively few sensational arrests, he had acquired an outstanding reputation in the field of tracing stolen property, and incidentally in pursuit of this specialty had earned a large number of insurance company rewards which might have encouraged the kindhearted observer to list a very human jealousy among the chief causes of his unpopularity. But apart from this plausible explanation there were even more human reasons why Lieutenant Corrio had so conspicuously failed to make himself the darling of Centre Street—he was a very smug man about his successes, and he had other vanities which were even less calculated to endear him to the other detectives whom his inspired brilliance had more than once put in the shade.

None of these things, however, were sufficient to

justify his immediate superiors in administering the official flattening which they had long been yearning to bestow; and it was with some pardonable glow of satisfaction that Inspector John Fernack, who was as human as anyone else if not more so, had at last found the adequate excuse for which his soul had been pining wistfully for many moons.

For at last Lieutenant Corrio's smug zeal had overreached itself. He had made an entirely gratuitous, uncalled for and unauthorized statement to a reporter on the New York *Daily Mail,* which had been featured under two-column headlines and decorated with Lieutenant Corrio's favourite photograph of himself on the first inside sheet of that enterprising tabloid.

This copy of the paper lay on Inspector Fernack's desk while he spoke his mind to his subordinate, and he referred to it several times for the best quotations which he had marked off in blue pencil in preparation for the interview.

One of these read: "If you ask me why this man Simon Templar was ever allowed to come back to New York, I can't tell you. I don't believe in idealistic crooks any more than I believe in reformed crooks, and the Police Department has got enough work to do without having any more hoodlums of that kind spilled onto us. But I can tell you this. There have been a lot of changes in the Detective Bureau since Templar was last here, and he won't find it so easy to get away with his racket as he did before."

There was another one: "If this cheap gunman that they call the Saint doesn't believe me, he's only got to start something. I'm taking care of him myself, and if he pulls so much as a traffic violation while he's in the city I'll get him put away where he won't give anyone any more trouble."

Fernack read out these extracts in his most scorching voice, which was a very scorching voice when he put his heart into it.

"I hadn't heard the news about your bein' appointed Police Commissioner," Fernack said heavily, "but I'd like to be the first to congratulate you. Of course a guy with your looks will find it a pretty soft job."

Lieutenant Corrio shrugged his shoulders sullenly. He was a dark and rather flashily good-looking man, who obviously had no illusions about the latter quality, with a wispy moustache and the slimmest figure consistent with the physical requirements of the force.

"I was just having a friendly chat with a guy," he said. "How was I to know he was going to print what I said? I didn't know anything about it until I saw it in the paper myself."

Fernack turned to page eleven and read out from another of his blue-pencilled panels: "Lieutenant Corrio is the exact reverse of the popular conception of a detective. He is a slender, well-dressed man who looks rather like Clark Gable and might easily be mistaken for an idol of the silver screen."

"You didn't know that he'd say that either, did you?" Fernack inquired in tones of acid that would have seared the skin of a rhinoceros.

Corrio glowered and said nothing; and Fernack passed on to what was to his mind the brightest and juiciest feature of the *Daily Mail* reporter's story. He read it out:

"After I left Lieutenant Corrio, it occurred to me to find out what Simon Templar thought about the subject.

"I found him without any difficulty in his suite

at the Waldorf. The Robin Hood of the modern underworld, who was once the favourite target of gangsters and police alike on account of his ruthless free-lance campaign against the criminals whom the law could not or would not touch, listened with his laziest smile while I read over Lieutenant Corrio's statements to him.

"I asked him if he had any answer to make.

"The Saint uncoiled his six feet two of steel-and-leathery length from the armchair where he had been sitting, and his clear blue eyes twinkled maliciously as he showed me to the door.

" 'I think Lieutenant Corrio will put Clark Gable out of business one of these days,' he said."

If there was anything that could have been guaranteed to increase Inspector Fernack's long-established secret sympathy for the Saint, it was this climax of a quotation. It is true that he would have preferred to have originated it himself, but the other compensations far outweighed this minor disadvantage.

Lieutenant Corrio's face reddened. He was particularly proud of his presidency of the Merrick Maskers, and he had never been able to see anything humourous in his confirmed conviction that his destined home was in Hollywood and that his true vocation was that of the dashing hero of a box-office-shattering series of romantic melodramas.

Having dealt comprehensively with these lighter points Fernack opened his shoulders and proceeded to the meatier business of the conference in a series of well-chosen sentences. He went on to summarize his opinion of Lieutenant Corrio's ancestry, past life, present value, future prospects, looks, clothes, morals, intelligence and assorted shortcomings, taking a point of view which made up in positiveness and vigour for anything which it may have lacked in absolute impartiality.

"An' get this," he concluded. "The Saint hasn't come here to get into any trouble. I know him an' he knows me, an' he knows me too damn well to try to pull anything while I'm still gettin' around on my own feet. An' what's more, if anybody's got to take care of him I can do it. He's a man-sized proposition, an' it takes a man-sized cop to look after him. An' if any statements have to made to the papers about it, I'll make 'em."

Corrio waited for the storm to pass its height, which took some time longer.

"I'm sure you know best, sir—especially after the way he helped you on that Valcross case," he said humbly, while Fernack glared at him speechlessly. "But I have a theory about the Saint."

"You have a what?" repeated Fernack as if Corrio had uttered an indecent word.

"A theory, sir. I think the mistake that's been made all along is in trying to get something on the Saint *after* he's done a job. What we ought to do is pick out a job that he looks likely to do, watch it, and catch him redhanded. After all, his character is so well known that any real detective ought to be able to pick out the things that would interest him with his eyes shut. There's one in that paper on your desk—I noticed it this morning."

"Are you still talking about this?" Fernack demanded unsympathetically. "Because if so—"

Corrio shook his head.

"I mean that man Oppenheim who owns the sweatshops. It says in the paper that he's just

bought the Vanderwoude emerald collection for a
million and a half dollars to give to his daughter
for a wedding present. Knowing how Oppenheim
got his money, and knowing the Saint's line, it's my
idea that the Saint will make a play for those
jewels."

"An' make such a sucker play that even a fairy
like you could catch him at it," snarled Fernack
discouragingly. "Go back and do your detecting at
the Merrick Playhouse—I hear there's a bad ham
out there they've been trying to find for some
time."

If he had been less incensed with his subordinate
Fernack might have perceived a germ of sound
logic in Corrio's theory, but he was in no mood to
appreciate it. Two days later he did not even remember that the suggestion had been made; which
was an oversight on his part, for it was at that time
that Simon Templar did indeed develop a serious
interest in the unpleasant Mr. Oppenheim.

This was because Janice Dixon stumbled against
him late one night as he was walking home along
Forty-eighth Street in the dark and practically
deserted block between Sixth and Seventh Avenues. He had to catch her to save her from falling.

"I'm sorry," she muttered.

He murmured some absent-minded commonplace and straightened her up, but her weight
was still heavy on his hand. When he let her go she
swayed towards him and clung onto his arm.

"I'm sorry," she repeated stupidly.

His first thought was that she was drunk, but her
breath was innocent of the smell of liquor. Then he
thought the accident might be only the excuse for a
more mercenary kind of introduction, but he saw

her face was not made up as he would have expected it to be in that case. It was a pretty face, but so pale that it looked ghostly in the semi-darkness between the far-spaced street lamps; and he saw that she had dark circles under her eyes and that her mouth was without lipstick.

"Is anything the matter?" he asked.

"No—it's nothing. I'll be all right in a minute. I just want to rest."

"Let's go inside somewhere and sit down."

There was a drugstore on the corner and he took her into it. It seemed to be a great effort for her to walk and another explanation of her unsteadiness flashed into his mind. He sat her down at the counter and ordered two cups of coffee.

"Would you like something to eat with it?"

Her eyes lighted up and she bit her lip.

"Yes. I would. But—I haven't any money."

"I shouldn't worry about that. We can always hold up a bank." The Saint watched her while she devoured a sandwich, a double order of bacon and eggs and a slice of pie. She ate intently, quickly, without speaking. Without seeming to stare at her, his keen eyes took in the shadows under her cheekbones, the neat patch on one elbow of the cheap dark coat, the cracks in the leather of shoes which had long since lost their shape.

"I wish I had your appetite," he said gently, when at last she had finished.

She smiled for the first time, rather faintly.

"I haven't had anything to eat for two days," she said. "And I haven't had as much to eat as this all at once for a long time."

Simon ordered more coffee and offered her a cigarette. He put his heels upon the top rung of his stool and leaned his elbows on his knees. She told him her name, but for the moment he didn't answer with his own.

"Out of a job?" he asked quietly.

She shook her head.

"Not yet."

"You aren't on a diet by any chance, are you?"

"Yes. A nice rich diet of doughnuts and coffee, mostly." She smiled rather wearily at his puzzlement. "I work for Oppenheim."

"Doesn't he pay you?"

"Sure. But maybe you haven't heard of him. I'm a dressmaker. I work with fifty other girls in a loft down near the East River, making handmade underwear. We work ten hours a day, six days a week, sewing. If you're clever and fast you can make two pieces in a day. They pay you thirty cents apiece. You can buy them on Fifth Avenue for four or five dollars, but that doesn't do us any good. I made three dollars last week, but I had to pay the rent for my room."

It was Simon Templar's first introduction to the economics of the sweatshop; and hardened as he was to the ways of chiselers and profiteers, the cold facts as she stated them made him feel slightly sick to his stomach. He realized that he had been too long in ignorance of the existence of such people as Mr. Oppenheim.

"Do you mean to say he gets people to work for him on those terms?" he said incredulously. "And how is it possible to live on three dollars a week?"

"Oh, there are always girls who'll do it if they can't get anything else. I used to get forty dollars a week doing the same work on Madison Avenue, but I was sick for a couple of weeks and they used it as an excuse to let me go. I didn't have any job at all for three months, and three dollars a week is better than nothing. You learn how to live on it. After a while you get used to being hungry; but when you have to buy shoes or pay a dentist's bill, and the rent piles up for a couple of weeks, it doesn't do you any good."

"I seem to have heard of your Mr. Oppenheim," said the Saint thoughtfully. "Didn't he just pay a million and a half dollars for a collection of emeralds?"

Her lips flickered cynically.

"That's the guy. I've seen them, too—I've been working on his daughter's trousseau because I've got more experience of better-class work than the other girls, and I've been going to the house to fit it. It's just one of those things that make you feel like turning communist sometimes."

"You've been in the house, have you?" he said even more thoughtfully. "And you've seen these emeralds?" He stopped himself and drew smoke from his cigarette to trickle it thoughtfully back across the counter. When he turned to her again, his dark reckless face held only the same expression of friendly interest that it had held before. "Where are you going to sleep tonight?"

She shrugged.

"I don't know. You see, I owe three weeks' rent now, and they won't let me in until I pay it. I guess I'll take a stroll up to the park."

"It's healthy enough, but a bit drafty." He smiled at her suddenly with disarming frankness. "Look here, what would you say if I suggested that we wander around to a little place close by here where I can get you a room? It's quiet and clean, and I don't live there. But I'd like to do something about you. Stay there tonight and meet me for dinner tomorrow, and let's talk it over."

She met him the following evening, and he had to do very little more than keep his ears open to learn everything that he wanted to know.

"They're in Oppenheim's study—on the second floor. His daughter's room is next door to it, and the walls aren't very thick. He was showing them to her yesterday afternoon when I was there. He has a big safe in the study, but he doesn't keep the emeralds in it. I heard him boasting about how clever he was. He said, 'Anybody who came in looking for the emeralds would naturally think they'd be in the safe, and they'd get to work on it at once. It'd take them a long time to open it, which would give us plenty of chances to catch them; but anyhow they'd be disappointed. They'd never believe that I had a million and a half dollars' worth of emeralds just tucked away behind a row of books on a shelf. Even the man from the detective agency doesn't know it—he thinks the safe is what he's got to look after.' "

"So they have a private detective on the job, do they?" said the Saint.

"Yes. A man from Ingerbeck's goes in at seven o'clock every evening and stays till the servants are up in the morning. The butler's a pretty tough-looking guy himself, so I suppose Oppenheim thinks the house is safe enough in his hands in the daytime. . . . Why do you want to know all this?"

"I'm interested."

She looked at him with an unexpected clearness of understanding.

"Is that what you meant when you said you'd

like to do something about me? Did you think you could do it if you got hold of those emeralds?"

The Saint lighted a cigarette with a steady and unhurried hand, and then his blue eyes came back to her face for a moment before he answered with a very quiet and calculating directness.

"That was more or less my idea," he said calmly.

She was neither shocked nor frightened. She studied him with as sober and matter-of-fact attention as if they were discussing where she might find another job, but a restrained intenseness with which he thought he could sympathize came into her voice. She said: "I couldn't call anybody a criminal who did that. He really deserves to lose them. I believe I'd be capable of robbing him myself if I knew how to go about it. Have you ever done anything like that before?"

"I have had a certain amount of experience," Simon admitted mildly.

"Who are you?"

"If you were reading newspapers a few years back you may have read about me. I'm called the Saint."

"You? You're kidding." She stared at him, and the amused disbelief in her face changed slowly into a weakening incredulity. "But you might be. I saw a photograph once . . . Oh, if you only were! I'd help you to do it—I wouldn't care what it cost."

"You can help me by telling me everything you can remember about Oppenheim's household and how it works."

She had been there several times; and there were many useful things she remembered, which his skillful questioning helped to bring out. They went down into the back of his mind and stayed there while he talked about other things. The supremely simple and obvious solution came to him a full two hours later, when they were dancing on a small packed floor above Broadway.

He took her back to their table as the main batteries of lights went on for the floor show, lighted a cigarette and announced serenely:

"It's easy. I know just how Comrade Oppenheim is going to lose his emeralds."

"How?"

"They have a man in from Ingerbeck's at night, don't they? And he has the run of the place while everybody else is asleep. They give him breakfast in the morning when the servants get up, and then he takes a cigar and goes home. Well, the same thing can happen just once more. The guy from Ingerbeck's comes in, stays the night and goes home. Not the usual guy, because he's sick or been run over by a truck or something. Some other guy. And when this other guy goes home, he can pull emeralds out of every pocket."

Her mouth opened a little.

"You mean you'd do that?"

"Sure. Apart from the fact that I don't like your Mr. Oppenheim, it seems to me that with a million and a half dollars' worth of emeralds one could do a whole lot of amusing things which Oppenheim would never dream of. To a bloke with my imagination—"

"But when would you do it?"

He looked at his watch mechanically.

"Eventually—why not now? Or at least this evening." He was almost mad enough to consider it, but he restrained himself. "But I'm afraid it might be asking for trouble. It'll probably take me a day or two to find out a few more things about this dick from Ingerbeck's, and then I'll have to get organized to keep him out of the way on the night I want to go in. I should think you could call it a date for Friday."

She nodded with a queer childish gravity.

"I believe you'd do it. You sound very sure of everything. But what would you do with the emeralds after you got them?"

"I expect we could trade them in for a couple of hamburgers—maybe more."

"You couldn't sell them."

"There are ways and means."

"You couldn't sell stones like that. I'm sure you couldn't. Everything in a famous collection like that would be much too well known. If you took them into a dealer he'd recognize them at once, and then you'd be arrested."

The Saint smiled. It has never been concealed from the lynx-eyed student of these chronicles that Simon Templar had his own very human weaknesses; and one of these was very much akin to the one which had contributed so generously to the unpopularity of Lieutenant Corrio. If the Saint made himself considerably less ridiculous with it, it was because he was a very different type of man. But the Saint had his own deeply planted vanities; and one of these was a deplorable weakness of resistance to the temptation to display his unique knowledge of the devious ways of crime, like a peddler spreading his wares in the market place before a suitably impressed and admiring audience.

"Three blocks north of here, on Fifty-second Street," he said, "there's a little bar where you can find the biggest fence in the United States any evening between five and eight o'clock. He'll take anything you like to offer him across the table, and pay top prices for it. You could sell him the English crown jewels if you had them. If I borrow Oppenheim's emeralds on Friday night I'll be rid of them by dinnertime Saturday, and then we'll meet for a celebration and see where you'd like to go for a vacation."

He was in high spirits when he took her home much later to the lodginghouse where he had found her a room the night before. There was one virtue in the indulgence of his favorite vice: talking over the details of a coup which he was freshly planning in his mind helped him to crystallize and elaborate his own ideas, gave him a charge of confidence and optimistic energy from which the final strokes of action sprung as swiftly and accurately as bullets out of a gun. When he said good night to her he felt as serene and exhilarated in spirit as if the Vanderwoude emeralds were already his own. He was in such good spirits that he had walked a block from the lodginghouse before he remembered that he had left her without trying to induce her to take some money for her immediate needs, and without making any arrangement to meet her again.

He turned and walked back. Coincidence, an accident of time involving only a matter of seconds, had made incredible differences to his life before: this, he realized later, was only another of those occasions when an overworked guardian angel seemed to play with the clock to save him from disaster.

The dimly lighted desert of the hall was surrounded by dense oases of potted palms, and one of these obstructions was in a direct line from the front door, so that anyone who entered quietly might easily remain unnoticed until he had circumnavigated this clump of shrubbery. The Saint, who from the ingrained habit of years of dangerous living moved silently without conscious effort, was just preparing to step around this divinely inspired decoration when he heard someone speaking in the hall and caught the sound of a name which stopped him dead in his tracks. The name was Corrio. Simon stood securely hidden behind the fronds of imported vegetation and listened for as long as he dared to some of the most interesting lines of dialogue which he had ever overhead. When he had heard enough, he slipped out again as quietly as he had come in and went home without disturbing Janice Dixon. He would get in touch with her the next day; for the moment he had something much more urgent to occupy his mind.

It is possible that even Lieutenant Corrio's smugness might have been shaken if he had known about this episode of unpremeditated eavesdropping, but this unpleasant knowledge was hidden from him. His elastic self-esteem had taken no time at all to recover from the effects of Fernack's reprimand; and when Fernack happened to meet him on a certain Friday afternoon he looked as offensively sleek and self-satisfied as he had always been. It was beyond Fernack's limits of self-denial to let the occasion go by without making the use of it to which he felt he was entitled.

"I believe Oppenheim has still got his emeralds," he remarked with a certain feline joviality.

Lieutenant Corrio's glossy surface was unscratched.

"Don't be surprised if he doesn't keep them

much longer," he said. "And don't blame me if the Saint gets away with it. I gave you the tip once and you wouldn't listen."

"Yeah, you gave me the tip," Fernack agreed benevolently. "When are you goin' out to Holly-wood to play Sherlock Holmes?"

Maybe it won't be so long now," Corrio said darkly. "Paragon Pictures are pretty interested in me—apparently one of their executives happened to see me playing the lead in our last show at the Merrick Playhouse, and they want me to take a screen test."

Fernack grinned evilly.

"You're too late," he said. "They've already made a picture of *Little Women*."

He had reason to regret some of his jibes the next morning, when news came in that every single one of Mr. Oppenheim's emeralds had been removed from their hiding place and taken out of the house, quietly and without any fuss, in the pockets of a detective of whom the Ingerbeck Agency had never heard. They had, they said, been instructed by tele-phone that afternoon to discontinue the service, and the required written confirmation had arrived a few hours later, written on Mr. Oppenheim's own flowery letterhead and signed with what they firm-ly believed to be his signature; and nobody had been more surprised and indignant than they were when Mr. Oppenheim, on the verge of an apoplec-tic fit, had rung up Mr. Ingerbeck himself and de-manded to know how many more crooks they had on their payroll and what the blank blank they pro-posed to do about it. The imposter had arrived at the house at the usual hour in the evening, ex-plained that the regular man had been taken ill and presented the necessary papers to accredit himself; and he had been left all night in the study, and let out at breakfast time according to the usual custom. When he went out he was worth a million and a half dollars as he stood up. He was, according to the butler's rather hazy description, a tallish man with horn-rimmed glasses and a thick crop of red hair.

"That red hair and glasses is all baloney," said Corrio, who was in Fernack's office when the news came in. "Just an ordinary wig and a pair of frames from any optician's. It was the Saint all right—you can see his style right through it. What did I tell you?"

"What th' hell d'ya think you can tell *me?*" Fernack roared back at him. Then he subdued himself. "Anyway, you're crazy. The Saint's out of business."

Corrio shrugged.

"Would you like me to take the case, sir?"

"What, you?" Fernack paused to take careful aim at the cuspidor. "I'll take the case myself." He glowered at Corrio thoughtfully for a moment. "Well, if you know so much about it, you can come along with me. And we'll see how smart you are."

Ten minutes later they were in a taxi on their way to Oppenheim's house.

It was a silent journey, for Fernack was too full of a vague sort of wrath to speak, and Corrio seemed quite content to sit in a corner and finger his silky moustache with an infuriatingly tranquil air of being quite well satisfied with the forthcoming opportunity of demonstrating his own brilliance.

In the house they found a scene of magnificent

confusion. There was the butler, who seemed to be getting blamed for having admitted the thief; there was a representative of Ingerbeck's, whose temper appeared to be fraying rapidly under the flood of wild accusations which Oppenheim was flinging at him; there was a very suave and imperturbable official of the insurance company which had covered the jewels; and there was Mr. Oppenheim himself, a short fat yellow-faced man, dancing about like an agitated marionette, shaking his fists in an ecstasy of rage, screaming at the top of his voice, and accusing everybody in sight of crimes and perversions which would have been worth at least five hundred years in Sing Sing if they could have been proved. Fernack and Corrio had to listen while he unburdened his soul again from the beginning.

"And now vat you think?" he wound up. "These dirty crooks, this insurance company vat takes all my money, they say they don't pay anything. They say they repudiate the policy. Just because I tried to keep the emeralds vere they couldn't be found, instead of leaving them in a safe vat anyone can open."

"The thing is," explained the official of the insurance company, with his own professional brand of unruffled unctuousness, "that Mr. Oppenheim has failed to observe the conditions of the policy. It was issued on the express understanding that if the emeralds were to be kept in the house, they were to be kept in this safe and guarded by a detective from some recognized agency. Neither of these stipulations have been complied with, and in the circumstances—"

"It's a dirty svindle!" shrieked Oppenheim. "Vat do I care about your insurance company? I vill cancel all my policies. I buy up your insurance company and throw you out in the street to starve. I offer my own reward for the emeralds. I vill pay half a mil—I mean a hundred thousand dollars to the man who brings back my jewels!"

"Have you put that in writing yet?" asked Lieu-tentant Corrio quickly.

"No. But I do so at vonce. Bah! I vill show these dirty double-crossing crooks . . ."

He whipped out his fountain pen and scurried over to the desk.

"Here, wait a minute," said Fernack, but Op-penheim paid no attention to him. Fernack turned to Corrio. "I suppose you've gotta be sure of the reward before you start showin' us how clever you are," he said nastily.

"No sir. But we have to consider the theory that the robbery might have been committed with that in mind. Emeralds like those would be difficult to dispose of profitably—I can only think of one fence in the East who'd handle a package of stuff like that."

"Then why don't you pull him in?" snapped Fernack unanswerably.

"Because I've never had enough evidence. But I'll take up that angle this afternoon."

He took no further part in the routine examina-tions and questionings which Fernack conducted with dogged efficiency, but on the way back to Centre Street he pressed his theory again with un-usual humility.

"After all, sir," he said, "we've all known for a long time that there's one fence in the East who'll handle anything that's brought him, however big it is. I've been working on him quietly for a long time, and I'm pretty certain who it is, though I've never been able to get anything on him. I even know where he can be found and where he does most of his buying, and I don't mind telling you that it's helped me a lot in tracing the loot from other jobs. Even if this isn't one of the Saint's jobs, whoever did it, there are only four things they can do with the emeralds. They can hold them for the reward, they can cut them up and sell them as small stuff, they can try to smuggle them out of the country or they can just get rid of them in one shot to this guy I've got in mind. Of course they may be planning any of the first three things, but they may just as well be planning the fourth, and we aren't justified in overlooking it. And if we're going to do anything about it, we've got to do it pretty quickly. I know you don't think much of me, sir," said Corrio with unwonted candour, "but you must admit that I was right a few days ago when you wouldn't listen to me, and now I think it'd be only fair for you to give me another chance."

Almost against his will Fernack forced himself to be just.

"All right," he said grudgingly. "Where do we find this guy?"

"If you can be free about a quarter to five this afternoon," said Corrio, "I'd like you to come along with me."

Simon Templar walked west along Fifty-second Street. He felt at peace with the world. At such times as this he was capable of glowing with a vast and luxurious contentment, the same deep and satisfying tranquillity that might follow a perfect meal eaten in hunger or the drinking of a cool drink at the end of a hot day. As usually happened with him, this mood had made its mark on his clothes. He had dressed himself with some care for the occasion in one of the most elegant suits and brightly colored shirts from his extensive wardrobe, and he was a very beautiful and resplendent sight as he sauntered along the sidewalk with the brim of his hat tilted piratically over his eyes, looking like some swashbuckling medieval brigand who had been miraculously transported into the twentieth century and put into modern dress without losing the swagger of a less inhibited age. In one hand he carried a brown paper parcel.

Fernack's huge fist closed on his arm near the corner of Seventh Avenue, and the Saint looked around and recognized him with a delighted and completely innocent smile.

"Why, hullo there," he murmured. "The very man I've been looking for." He discovered Corrio coming up out of the background and smiled again. "Hi, Gladys," he said politely.

Corrio seized his other arm and worked him swiftly and scientifically into a doorway. Corrio kept one hand in his side pocket, and whatever he had in his pocket prodded against the Saint's stomach and kept him pinned in a corner. There was a gleam of excitement in his dark eyes. "I guess my hunch was right again," he said to Fernack.

Fernack kept his grip of the Saint's arm. His frosted grey eyes glared at the Saint angrily, but not with the sort of anger that most people would have expected.

"You damn fool," he said rather damn-foolishly. "What did you have to do it for? I told you when you came over that you couldn't get away with that stuff any more."

"What stuff?" asked the Saint innocently.

Corrio had grabbed the parcel out of his hand and he was tearing it open with impatient haste.

"I guess this is what we're looking for," he said.

The broken string and torn brown paper fluttered to the ground as Corrio ripped them off. When the outer wrappings were gone he was left with a cardboard box. Inside the box there was a layer of crumpled tissue paper. Corrio jerked it out and remained staring frozenly at what was finally exposed. This was a fully dressed and very lifelike doll with features that were definitely familiar. Tied around its neck on a piece of ribbon was a ticket on which was printed: "Film Star Series, No. 12: CLARK GABLE. 69c."

An expression of delirious and incredulous relief began to creep over the harsh angles of Fernack's face—much the same expression as might have come into the face of a man who, standing close by the crater of a rumbling volcano, had seen it suddenly explode only to throw off a shower of fairy lights and coloured ballons. The corners of his mouth began to twitch, and a deep vibration like the tremor of an approaching earthquake began to quiver over his chest; then suddenly his mouth opened to let out a shout of gargantuan laughter like the bellow of a joyful bull.

Corrio's face was black with fury. He tore out the rest of the packing paper and squeezed out every scrap of it between his fingers, snatched the doll out of the box and twisted and shook it to see if anything could have been concealed inside it. Then he flung that down also among the mounting fragments of litter on the ground. He thrust his face forward until it was within six inches of the Saint's.

"Where are they?" he snarled savagely.

"Where are who?" asked the Saint densely.

"You know damn well what I'm talking about," Corrio said through his teeth. "What have you done with the stuff you stole from Oppenheim's last night? Where are the Vanderwoude emeralds?"

"Oh, them," said the Saint mildly. "That's a funny question for *you* to ask." He leaned lazily on the wall against which Corrio had forced him, took out his cigarette case and looked at Fernack.

"As a matter of fact," he said calmly, "that's what I wanted to see you about. If you're particularly interested I think I could show you where they went to."

The laugh died away on Fernack's lips, to be replaced by the startled and hurt look of a dog that has been given an unexpected bone and then kicked almost as soon as it has picked it up.

"So you do know something about that job," he said slowly.

"I know plenty," said the Saint. "Let's take a cab."

He straightened up off the wall. For a moment Corrio looked as if he would pin him back there, but Fernack's intent interest countermanded the movement without speaking or even looking at him. Fernack was puzzled and disturbed, but somehow the Saint's quiet voice and unsmiling eyes told him that there was something there to be taken seriously. He stepped back, and Simon walked past him unhindered and opened the door of a taxi standing by the curb.

"Where are we going to?" Fernack asked, as they turned south down Fifth Avenue.

The Saint grinned gently and settled back in his

corner with his cigarette. He ignored the question.

"Once upon a time," he said presently, "there was a smart detective. He was very smart because after some years of ordinary detecting he had discovered that the main difficulty about the whole business was that you often have to find out who committed a crime, and since criminals don't usually leave their names and addresses behind them this is liable to mean a lot of hard work and a good many disappointments. Besides which, the pay of a police lieutenant isn't nearly so big as that amount of brainwork seems to deserve. So this guy, being a smart fellow, thought of a much simpler method, which was more or less to persuade the criminals to tell him about it themselves. Of course, he couldn't arrest them even then, because if he did that they might begin to suspect that he had some ulterior motive; but there were plenty of other ways of making a deal out of it. For instance, suppose a crook got away with a tidy cargo of loot and didn't want to put it away in the refrigerator for icicles to grow on; he could bring his problem to our smart detective, and our smart detective could think it over and say, 'Well, Elmer, that's pretty easy. All you do is just go and hide this loot in an ash can on Second Avenue or hang it on a tree in Central Park, or something like that, and I'll do a very smart piece of detecting and find it. Then I'll collect the reward and we'll go shares in it.' Usually this was pretty good business for the crook, the regular fences being as miserly as they are, and the detective didn't starve on it either. Of course the other detectives in the bureau weren't so pleased about it, being jealous of seeing this same guy collecting such a lot of credits and fat insurance company checks; but somehow it never seemed to occur to them to wonder how he did it."

He finished speaking as the taxi drew up at an apartment hotel near the corner of East Twelfth Street.

Fernack was sitting forward, with his jaw square and hard and his eyes fixed brightly on the Saint's face.

"Go on," he said gruffly.

"We'll change the scene again."

He got out and paid off the driver and the other two followed him into the hotel. Corrio's face seemed to have gone paler under its olive tan.

Simon paused in the lobby and glanced at him.

"Will you ask for the key, or shall I? It might be better if you asked for it," he said softly, "because the clerk will recognize you. Even if he doesn't know you by your right name."

"I don't quite know what you're talking about," Corrio said coldly, "but if you think you can wriggle out of this with any of your wild stories, you're wasting your time." He turned to Fernack. "I have got an apartment here, sir—I just use it sometimes when I'm kept in town late and I can't get home. It isn't in my own name, because—well, sir, you understand—I don't always want everybody to know who I am. This man has got to know about it somehow, and he's just using it to try and put up some crazy story to save his own skin."

"All the same," said Fernack with surprising gentleness, "I'd like to go up. I want to hear some more of this crazy story."

Corrio turned on his heel and went to the desk. The apartment was on the third floor—an ordinary two-room suite with the usual revolting furniture to be found in such places. Fernack glanced briefly over the living room into which they entered and looked at the Saint again.

"Go on," he said. "I'm listening."

The Saint sat down on the edge of the table and blew smoke rings.

"It would probably have gone on a lot longer," he said, "if this smart detective hadn't thought one day what a supremely brilliant idea it would be to combine business with profit, and have the honour of convicting a most notorious and elusive bandit known as the Saint—not forgetting, of course, to collect the usual cash reward in the process. So he used a very goodlooking young damsel—you ought to meet her sometime, Fernack, she really is a peach—having some idea that the Saint would never run away very fast from a pretty face. In which he was damn right . . . She had a very well-planned hardluck story, too, and the whole act was most professionally staged. It had all the ingredients that a good psychologist would bet on to make the Saint feel that stealing Oppenheim's emeralds was the one thing he had left glaringly undone in an otherwise complete life. Even the spadework of the job had already been put in, so that she could practically tell the Saint how to pinch the jewels. So that our smart detective must have thought he was sitting pretty, with a sucker all primed to do the dirty work for him and take the rap if anything went wrong—besides being still there to take the rap when the smart detective made his arrest and earned the reward if everything went right."

Simon smiled dreamily at a particularly repulsive print on the wall for a moment.

"Unfortunately, I happened to drop in on this girl one time when she wasn't expecting me, and I heard her phoning a guy named Corrio to tell him I was well and truly hooked," he said. "On account of having read in the *Daily Mail* some talk by a guy of the same name about what he was going to do to me, I was naturally interested."

Corrio started forward.

"Look here, you—"

"Wait a minute." Fernack held him back with an iron arm. "I want the rest of it. Did you do the job, Saint?"

Simon shook his head sadly. It was at that point that his narrative departed, for the very first time, from the channels of pure veracity in which it had begun its course—but Fernack was not to know this.

"Would I be such a sap?" he asked reproachfully. "I knew I could probably get away with the actual robbery because Corrio would want me to; but as soon as it was over, knowing in advance who'd done it, he'd be chasing round to catch me and recover the emeralds. So I told the girl I'd thought it all over and decided I was too busy." The Saint sighed as if he was still regretting a painful sacrifice. "The rest is pure theory; but this girl gave me a checkroom ticket on Grand Central this morning and asked me if I'd collect a package on it this afternoon and take it along to an address on Fifty-second Street. I didn't do it because I had an idea what would happen; but my guess would be that if somebody went along and claimed the parcel they'd find emeralds in it. Not all the emeralds, probably, because that'd be too risky if I got curious and opened it; but some of them. The rest are probably here—I've been looking around since we've been here, and I think there's some new and rather amateurish stitching in the upholstery of that chair. I could do something with that reward myself."

Corrio barred his way with a gun as he got off the table.

"You stay where you are," he grated. "If you're trying to get away with some smart frame-up—"

Simon looked down at the gun.

"You talk altogether too much," he said evenly. "And I don't think you're going to be safe with that toy in a minute."

He hit Corrio very suddenly under the chin, grabbing the gun with his other hand as he did so. The gun went off crashingly as Corrio reeled backwards, but after that it remained in the Saint's hand. Corrio stood trembling against the wall, and Simon looked at Fernack again and rubbed his knuckles thoughtfully.

"Just to make sure," he said, "I fixed a dictagraph under the table yesterday. Let's see if it has anything to say."

Fernack watched him soberly as he prepared to play back the record. In Fernack's mind was the memory of a number of things which he had heard Corrio say which fitted into the picture which the Saint offered him much too vividly to be easily denied.

Then the dictagraph record began to play. And Fernack felt a faint shiver run up his spine at the uncannily accurate reproduction of Corrio's voice.

"Smart work, Leo . . . I'll say these must be worth every penny of the price on them."

The other voice was unfamiliar.

"Hell, it was a cinch. The layout was just like you said. But how you goin' to fix it on the other guy?"

"That's easy. The broad gets him to fetch a parcel from Grand Central and take it where I tell her to tell him. When he gets there, I'm waiting for him."

"You're not goin' to risk givin' him all that stuff?"

"Oh, don't be so thick. There'll only be just enough in the parcel to frame him. Once he's caught, it'll be easy enough to plant the rest somewhere and find it."

Corrio's eyes were wide and staring.

"It's a plant!" he screamed hysterically. "That's a record of the scene I played in the film test I made yesterday."

Simon smiled politely, cutting open the up-holstery of the armchair and fishing about for a leather pouch containing about fourteen hundred thousand dollars' worth of emeralds which should certainly be there unless somebody else had found them since he chose that ideal hiding place for his loot.

"I only hope you'll be able to prove it, Gladys," he murmured, and watched Fernack grasp Corrio's arm with purposeful efficiency.

III   THE WELL-MEANING MAYOR

Sam purdell never quite knew how he became Mayor. He was a small and portly man with a round blank face and a round blank mind, who had built up a moderately profitable furniture business over the last thirty-five years and acquired in the process a round pudding-faced wife and a couple of suet dumplings of daughters; but the inexhaustible zeal for improving the circumstances and morals of the community, that fierce drive of ambition and the twitching of the ears for the ecstatic screams of *"Heil"* whenever he went abroad, that indomitable urge to be a leader of his people from which Hitlers and Mussolinis are born, was not naturally in him.

It is true that at the local reform club, of which he was a prominent member, he had often been stimulated by an appreciative audience and a large highball to lay down his views on the way in which he thought everything on earth ought to be run, from Japanese immigration to the permissible percentage of sulphur dioxide in dried apricots; but there was nothing outstandingly indicative of a political future in that. This is a disease which is liable to attack even the most honest and respectable citizens in such circumstances. But the idea that he himself should ever occupy the position in which he might be called upon to put all those beautiful ideas into practice had never entered Sam Purdell's head in those simple early days; and if it had not been for the drive supplied by Al Eisenfeld, it might never have materialized.

"You ought to be in politics, Sam," Al had insisted, at the close of one of these perorations several years before.

Sam Purdell considered the suggestion.

"No, I wouldn't be clever enough," he said modestly.

To tell the truth, he had heard the suggestion before, had repudiated it before and had always wanted to hear it contradicted. Al Eisenfeld obliged him. It was the first time anybody had been so obliging.

This was three years before the columnist of the *Elmford News* was moved to inquire:

"How long does our mayor think he can kid reporters and deputations with his celebrated pose of injured innocence?

"We always thought it was a good act while it lasted; but isn't it time we had a new show?"

It was not the first time that it had been suggested in print that the naive and childlike simplicity which was Sam Purdell's greatest charm was one of the shrewdest fronts for ingenious corruption which any politician had ever tried to put over a batch of sane electors, but this was the nearest that any commentator had ever dared to come to saying that Sam Purdell was a crook.

It was a suggestion which left Sam a pained and puzzled man. He couldn't understand it. These adopted children of his, these citizens whose weal occupied his mind for twenty-four hours a day, were turning round to bite the hand that fed them. And the unkindest cut of all, the blow which struck at the roots of his faith in human gratitude, was that he had only tried to do his best for the city which had been delivered into his care.

For instance, there was the time when, dragged forth by the energy of one of his rotund daughters, he had climbed laboriously one Sunday afternoon to the top of the range of hills which shelter Elmford on the north. When he had got his wind and started looking round, he realized that from that vantage point there was a view which might have rejoiced the heart of any artist. Sam Purdell was no artist, but he blinked with simple pleasure at the panorama of rolling hills and wooded groves with the river winding between them like the track of a great silver snail; and when he came home again he had a beautiful idea.

"You know, we got one of the finest views in the state up there on those hills! I never saw it before, and I bet you didn't either. And why? Because there ain't no road goes up there; and when you get to my age it ain't so easy to go scrambling up through those trees and brush."

"So what?" asked Al Eisenfeld, who was even less artistic and certainly more practical.

"So I tell you what we do," said Sam, glowing with the ardour of his enthusiasm almost as much as with the aftereffects of his unaccustomed exercise. "We build a highway up there so they can drive out in their automobiles week ends and look around comfortably. It makes work for a lot of men, and it don't cost too much; and everybody in Elmford can get a lot of free pleasure out of it.

Why, we might even get folks coming from all over the country to look at our view."

He elaborated this inspiration with spluttering eagerness, and before he had been talking for more than a quarter of an hour he had a convert.

"Sure, this is a great idea, Sam," agreed Mr. Eisenfeld warmly. "You leave it to me. Why, I know —we'll call it the Purdell Highway. . . ."

* * *

The Purdell Highway duly came into being at a cost of four million dollars. Al Eisenfeld saw to it. In the process of pushing Sam Purdell up the political tree he had engineered himself into the strategic post of Chairman of the Board of Aldermen, a position which gave him an interfering interest in practically all the activities of the city. The fact that the cost was about twice as much as the original estimate was due to the unforeseen obstinacy of the owner of the land involved, who held out for about four times the price which it was worth. There were rumours that someone in the administration had acquired the territory under another name shortly before the deal was proposed, and had sold it to the city at his own price—rumours which shocked Sam Purdell to the core of his sensitive soul.

"Do you hear what they say, Al?" he complained, as soon as these slanderous stories reached his ears. "They say I made one hundred thousand dollars graft out of the Purdell Highway! Now, why the hell should they say that?"

"You don't have to worry about what a few rats are saying, Sam," replied Mr. Eisenfeld soothingly. "They're only jealous because you're so popular with the city. Hell, there are political wranglers who'd tell stories about the Archangel Gabriel himself if he was Mayor, just to try and discredit

the administration so they could shove their own
crooked party in. I'll look into it.".

Mr. Eisenfeld's looking into it did not stop the
same rumours circulating about the Purdell Bridge,
which spanned the river from the southern end of
the town and linked it with the State Highway,
eliminating a detour of about twenty miles. What
project, Sam Purdell asked, could he possibly have
put forward that was more obviously designed for
the convenience and prosperity of Elmford? But
there were whispers that the Bennsville Steel Company, which had obtained the contract for the
bridge, had paid somebody fifty thousand dollars
to see that their bid was accepted. A bid which was
exactly fifty percent higher than the one put in by
their rivals.

"Do you know anything about somebody taking
fifty thousand dollars to put this bid through?" demanded Sam Purdell wrathfully, when he heard
about it; and Mr. Eisenfeld was shocked.

"That's a wicked idea, Sam," he protested. "Everyone knows this is the straightest administration
Elmford ever had. Why, if I thought anybody was
taking graft, I'd throw him out of the City Hall
with my own hands."

There were similar cases, each of which brought
Sam a little nearer to the brink of utter disillusion.
Sometimes he said that it was only the unshaken
loyalty of his family which stopped him from re-
signing his thankless labours and leaving Elmford
to wallow in its own ungrateful slime. But most of
all it was the loyalty and encouragement of Mr.
Eisenfeld.

Mr. Eisenfeld was a suave sleek man with none
of Sam Purdell's rubicund and open-faced geniali-
ty, but he had a cheerful courage in such trying

moments which was always ready to renew Sam
Purdell's faith in human nature. This cheerful
courage shone with its old unfailing luminosity
when Sam Purdell thrust the offending copy of the
Elmford News which we have already referred to
under Mr. Eisenfeld's aggrieved and incredulous
eyes.

"I'll show you what you do about that sort of
writing, Sam," said Mr. Eisenfeld magnificently.
"You just take it like this—"

He was going on to say that you tore it up, scat-
tering the libellous fragments disdainfully to the
four winds; but as he started to perform this heroic
gesture his eye was arrested by the next paragraph
in the same column, and he hesitated.

"Well, how do you take it?" asked the mayor
peevishly.

Mr. Eisenfeld said nothing for a second and the
mayor looked over his shoulder to see what he was
reading.

"Oh, that!" he said irritably. "I don't know what
that means. Do you know what it means, Al?"

"That" was a postscript about which Mr.
Purdell had some excuse to be puzzled.

"We hear that the Saint is back in this country.
People who remember what he did in New York a
couple of years ago might feel like inviting him to
take a trip out here. We can promise he would find
plenty of material on which to exercise his talents."

"What Saint are they talkin' about?" asked the
mayor. "I thought all the Saints were dead."

"This one isn't," said Mr. Eisenfeld; but for the
moment the significance of the name continued to
elude him. He had an idea that he had heard it before and that it should have meant something defi-
nite to him. "I think he was a crook who had a

great run in New York a while back. No, I remember it now. Wasn't he a sort of free-lance re-
former who had some crazy idea he could clean up
the city and put everything to rights . . .?"

He began to recall further details; and then as his
memory improved he closed the subject abruptly.
There were incidents among the stories that came
filtering back into his recollection which gave him
a vague discomfort in the pit of his stomach. It was
ridiculous, of course—a cheap journalistic
glorification of a common gangster; and yet, for
some reason, certain stories which he remembered
having read in the newspapers at the time made
him feel that he would be happier if the Saint's visit
to Elmford remained a theoretical proposition.

"We got lots of other more important things to
think about, Sam," he said abruptly, pushing the
newspaper into the wastebasket. "Look here—
about this monument of yours on the Elmford
Riviera . . ."

The Elmford Riviera was the latest and most
ambitious public work which the administration
had undertaken up to that date. It was to be the
crowning achievement in Sam Purdell's long list of
benevolences towards his beloved citizens.

A whole two miles of the riverbank had been acquired by the city and converted into a pleasure
park which the sponsors of the scheme claimed
would rival anything of its kind ever attempted in
the state. At one end of it a beautiful casino had
been erected where the citizens of Elmford might
gorge themselves with food, deafen themselves
with three orchestras and dance in tightly wedged
ecstasy till feet gave way. At the other end was to
be provided a children's playground, staffed with
trained attendants, where the infants of Elmford

might be left to bawl their heads off under the most expert and scientific supervision while their elders stopped to enjoy the adult amenities of the place. Behind the riverside drive, a concession had been arranged for an amusement park in which the populace could be shaken to pieces on roller coasters, whirled off revolving discs, thrown about in barrels, skittered over the falls and generally enjoy all the other elaborate forms of discomfort which help to make the modern seeker after relaxation so contemptuous of the unimaginative makeshift tortures which less enlightened souls had to get along with in medieval days. On the bank of the river itself, thousands of tons of sand had been imported to create an artificial beach where droves of holidaymakers could be herded together to blister and steam themselves into blissful imitations of the well-boiled prawn. It was, in fact, to be a place where Elmford might suffer all the horrors of Coney Island without the added torture of getting there.

And in the centre of this Elysian esplanade there was to be a monument to the man whose unquenchable devotion to the community had presented it with this last and most delightful blessing.

Sam Purdell had been modestly diffident about the monument, but Mr. Eisenfeld had insisted on it.

"You gotta have a monument, Sam," he had said. "The town owes it to you. Why, here you've been working for them all these years; and if you passed on tomorrow," said Mr. Eisenfeld, with his voice quivering at the mere thought of such a calamity, "what would there be to show for all you've done?"

"There's the Purdell Highway," said Sam deprecatingly, "the Purdell Suspension Bridge, the Purdell—"

"That's nothing," said Mr. Eisenfeld largely. "Those are just names. Why, in ten years after you die they won't mean any more than Grant or—or Pocahontas. What you oughta have is a monument of your own. Something with an inscription on it. I'll get the architect to design one."

The monument had duly been designed—a sort of square, tapering tower eighty feet high, crowned by an eagle with outspread wings, on the base of which was to be a great marble plaque on which the beneficence and public-spiritedness of Samuel Purdell would be recorded for all time. It was about the details of the construction of this monument that Mr. Eisenfeld had come to confer with the mayor.

"The thing is, Sam," he explained, "if this monument is gonna last, we gotta make it solid. They got the outside all built up now; but they say if we're gonna do the job properly, we got to fill it up with cement."

"That'll take an awful lot of cement, Al," Sam objected dubiously, casting an eye over the plans; but Mr. Eisenfeld's generosity was not to be balked.

"Well, what if it does? If the job's worth doin' at all, it's worth doin' properly. If you won't think of yourself, think of the city. Why, if we let this thing stay hollow and after a year or two it began to fall down, think what people from out of town would say."

"What would they say?" asked Mr. Purdell obtusely.

His adviser shuddered.

"They'd say this was such a cheap place we couldn't even afford to put up a decent monument for our mayor. You wouldn't like people to say a thing like that about us, would you, Sam?"

The mayor thought it over.

"Okay, Al," he said at length. "Okay. But I don't deserve it, really I don't."

Simon Templar would have agreed that the mayor had done nothing to deserve any more elaborate monument than a neat tombstone in some quiet worm cafeteria. But at that moment his knowledge of Elmford's politics was not so complete as it was very shortly to become.

When he saw Molly Provost slip the little automatic out of her bag he thought that the bullet was destined for the mayor; and in theory he approved. He had an engaging callousness about the value of political lives which, if universally shared, would make democracy an enchantingly simple business. But there were two policemen on motorcycles waiting to escort the mayoral car into the city, and the life of a good-looking girl struck him as being a matter for more serious consideration. He felt that if she were really determined to solve all of Elmford's political problems by shooting the mayor in the duodenum, she should at least be persuaded to do it on some other occasion when she would have a better chance of getting away with it. Wherefore the Saint moved very quickly, so that his lean brown hand closed over hers just at the moment when she touched the trigger and turned the bullet down into the ground.

Neither Sam Purdell nor Al Eisenfeld, who were climbing into the car at that moment, even so much as looked around; and the motorcycle escort mercifully joined with them in instinctively attributing the detonation to the backfire of a passing truck.

It was such a small gun that the Saint's hand easily covered it; and he held the gun and her hand together in a viselike grip, smiling as if he were just greeting an old acquaintance, until the wail of the sirens died away.

"Have you got a license to shoot mayors?" he inquired severely.

She had a small pale face which under a skillfully applied layer of cosmetics might have taken on a bright doll-like prettiness; but it was not like that yet. But he had a sudden illuminating vision of her face as it might have been, painted and powdered, with shaved eyebrows and blackened eyelashes, subtly hardened. It was a type which he had seen often enough before which he could recognize at once. Some of them he had seen happily married, bringing up adoring families; others . . . . For some reason the Saint thought that this girl ought not to be one of those others.

Then he felt her arm go limp, and took the gun out of her unresisting hand. He put it away in his pocket.

"Come for a walk," he said.

She shrugged dully.

"All right."

He took her arm and led her down the block. Around the corner, out of sight of the mayor's house, he opened the door of the first of a line of parked cars. She got in resignedly. As he let in the clutch and the car slipped away under the pull of a smoothly whispering engine, she buried her face in her hands and sobbed silently.

The Saint let her have it out. He drove on

thoughtfully, with a cigarette clipped between his lips, until the taller buildings of the business section rose up around them. In a quiet turning off one of the main streets of the town, he stopped the car outside a small restaurant and opened the door on her side to let her out.

She dabbed her eyes and straightened her hat mechanically. As she looked around and realized where they were, she stopped with one foot on the running board.

"What have you brought me here for?" she asked stupidly.

"For lunch," said the Saint calmly. "If you feel like eating. For a drink, if you don't. For a chat, anyhow."

She looked at him with fear and puzzlement still in her eyes.

"You needn't do that," she said steadily. "You can take me straight to the police station. We might as well get it over with."

He shook his head.

"Do you really want to go to a police station?" he drawled. "I'm not so fond of them myself, and usually they aren't very fond of me. Wouldn't you rather have a drink?"

Suddenly she realized that the smile with which he was looking down at her wasn't a bit like the grimly triumphant smile which a detective should have worn. Nor, when she looked more closely, was there anything else about him that quite matched her idea of what a detective would be like. It grieves the chronicler to record that her first impression was that he was too good-looking. But that was how she saw him. His tanned face was cut in a mould of rather reckless humour which didn't seem to fit in at all with the stodgy and prosaic backgrounds of the law. He was tall, and he looked strong—her right hand still ached from the steel grip of his fingers—but it was a supple kind of strength that had no connection with mere bulk. Also he wore his clothes with a gay and careless kind of elegance which no sober police chief could have approved. The twinkle in his eyes was wholly friendly.

"Do you mean you didn't arrest me just now?" she asked uncertainly.

"I never arrested anybody in my life," said the Saint cheerfully. "In fact, when they shoot politicians I usually give them medals. Come on in and let's talk."

Over a couple of martinis he explained himself further.

"My dear, I think it was an excellent scheme, on general principles. But the execution wasn't so good. When you've had as much experience in bumping people off as I have, you'll realize that it's no time to do it when a couple of cops are parked at the curb a few yards away. I suppose you realize that they would have got you just about ten seconds after you created a vacancy for a new mayor?"

She was still staring at him rather blankly.

"I wasn't trying to do anything to the mayor," she said. "It was Al Eisenfeld I was going to shoot, and I wouldn't have cared if they did get me afterwards."

The Saint frowned.

"You mean the seedy gigolo sort of bird who was with the mayor?"

She nodded.

"He's the real boss of the town. The mayor is just a figurehead."

"Other people don't seem to think he's as dumb as he looks," Simon remarked.

"They don't know. There's nothing wrong with Purdell, but Eisenfeld—"

"Maybe you have inside information," said the Saint.

She looked at him over her clenched fists, dry-eyed and defiant.

"If there were any justice in the world Al Eisenfeld would be executed."

The Saint raised his eyebrows and she read the thought in his mind and met it with cynical denial.

"Oh no—not in that way. There's no murder charge that anyone could bring against him. You couldn't bring any legal evidence in any court of law that he'd ever done any physical harm to anyone that I ever heard of. But I know that he is a murderer. He murdered my father."

And the Saint waited without interruption. The story came tumbling out in a tangle of words that bit into his brain with a burden of meaning that was one of the most profound and illuminating surprises that he had known for some considerable time. It was so easy to talk to him that before long he knew nearly as much as she did herself. He was such an easy and understanding listener that somehow it never seemed strange to her until afterwards that she had been pouring out so much to a man she had known for less than an hour. Perhaps it was not such an extraordinary story as such stories go—perhaps many people would have shrugged it away as one of the commonplace tragedies of a hard-boiled world.

"This fellow Schmidt was a pal of Eisenfeld's. So they tried to make Dad lay off him. Dad wouldn't listen to them. He was Police Commissioner before this administration came in and he'd never listened to any politicians in his life. He always said that he went into the force as an honest man, and he was going to stay that way. So when they found they couldn't keep him quiet, they framed him. They made out that he was behind practically every racket in the town. They did it cleverly enough. Dad knew they'd got him. He knew the game too well to be able to kid himself. He was booked to be thrown out of the force in disgrace—probably sent to jail as well. How could he hope to clear himself? The evidence which he had collected against Schmidt was in the District Attorney's office, but when Dad tried to bring that up they said that the safe had been burgled and it was gone. They even turned it around to make it look as if Dad had got rid of the evidence himself—the very thing he had told them he would never agree to do, so—I suppose he took the only way out that he could see. I suppose you'd say he was a coward to do it, but how could you ever know what he must have been suffering?"

"When was this?" asked the Saint quietly.

"Last night. He—shot himself. With his police gun. The shot woke me up. I—I found him. I suppose I must have gone mad too. I haven't slept since then—how could I? This morning I made up my mind. I came out to do the only thing that was left. I didn't care what happened to myself after that." She broke off helplessly. "Oh, I must have been crazy! But I couldn't think of anything else. Why should he be able to get away with it? Why should he?" she sobbed.

"Don't worry," said the Saint quietly. "He won't."

He spoke with a quiet and matter-of-fact certain-

ty which was more than a mere conventional encouragement. It made her look at him with a
perplexity which she had been able to forget while
he made her talk to him reawakening in her gaze.
For the first time since they had sat down, it
seemed, she was able to remember that she still
knew nothing about him; that he was no more than
a sympathetic stranger who had loomed up unheralded and unintroduced out of the fog which
had still not completely cleared from her mind.

"Of course you aren't a detective," she said
childishly. "I'd have recognized you if you were;
but you aren't, what are you?"

He smiled.

"I'm the guy who gives all the detectives something to work for," he said. "I'm the source of
more aches in the heads of the ungodly than I
should like to boast about. I am Trouble, In-
corporated—President Simon Templar, at your
service. They call me the Saint."

"What does that mean?" she asked helplessly.

In the ordinary way Simon Templar, who had no
spontaneous modesty bred into his composition,
would have felt a slight twinge of disappointment
that his reputation had not preceded him even to
that out-of-the-way corner of the American conti-
nent; but he realized that there was no legitimate
reason why she should have reacted more dramati-
cally to the revelation of his identity, and for once
he was not excessively discontented to remain un-
recognized. There were practical disadvantages to
the indulgence of this human weakness for publicity which, at that particular moment and in that
particular town, he was prepared to do without. He
shook his head with the same lazy grin that was so
extraordinarily comforting and clear-sighted.

"Nothing that you need worry about," he said. "Just write me down as a bloke who never could mind his own business, and give me some more of the inside dope about Al."

"There isn't a lot more to tell you," she said. "I think I've already given you almost everything I know."

"Doesn't anyone else in the town know it?"

"Hardly anybody. There are one or two people who guess how things really are, but if they tried to argue about it they'd only get laughed at. He's clever enough to have everybody believing that he's just Sam Purdell's mouthpiece; but it's the other way around. Sam Purdell really is dumb. He doesn't know what it's all about. He thinks of nothing but his highways and parks and bridges, and he honestly believes that he's only doing the best he can for the city. He doesn't get any graft out of it. Al gets all that; and he's clever enough to work it so that everybody thinks he's innocent and Sam Purdell is the really smart guy who's getting all the money out of it—even the Board of Aldermen think so. Dad used to talk to me about all his cases and he found out a lot about Eisenfeld while he was investigating this man Schmidt. He'd have gone after Eisenfeld himself next—if he'd been able to keep going. Perhaps Eisenfeld knew it and that made him more vicious."

"He didn't have any evidence against Eisenfeld?"

"Only a little. Hardly anything if you're talking about legal evidence, but he knew plenty of things he might have proven if he had been given time. That's how it is, anyway."

The Saint lighted a cigarette and gazed at her thoughtfully through a stream of smoke.

"You understood a lot more than I did, Molly," he murmured. "But it's a great idea . . . And the more I think of it, the more I think you must be right."

He let his mind play around with the situation for a moment. Maybe he was too subtle himself, but there was something about that fundamental master stroke of Mr. Eisenfeld's cunning that appealed to his incorrigible sense of the artistry of corruption. To be the power behind the scenes while some lifelike figurehead stood up to receive the rotten eggs was just ordinary astuteness. But to choose for that figurehead a man who was so honest and stupid that it would take an earthquake to make him realize what was going on, and whose honest stupidity might appear to less simple-minded inquirers as an impudent disguise for double-dyed villainy—that indicated a quality of guile to which Simon Templar raised an appreciative hat. But his admiration of Mr. Eisenfeld's ingenuity was purely theoretical.

He made a note of the girl's address.

"I'll keep the gun," he said before they parted. "You won't be needing it, and I shouldn't like you to lose your head again when I wasn't around to interfere." His blue eyes held her for a moment with quiet confidence. "Al Eisenfeld is going to be dealt with—I promise you that."

It was one of his many mysteries that the fantastic promise failed to rouse her to utter incredulity. Afterwards she would be incredulous, after he had fulfilled the promise even more so; but while she listened at that moment there was a spell about him which made all miracles seem possible.

"What can you do?" she asked, in the blind but indescribably inspiring belief that there must be some magic which he could achieve.

"I have my methods," said the Saint. "I stopped off here anyhow because I was interested in the stories I'd heard about this town, and we'll call it lucky that I happened to be out trying to take a look at the mayor when you had your brainstorm. Just do one thing for me. Whatever happens, don't tell a living soul about this lunch. Forget that you ever met me or heard of me. Let me do the remembering."

Mr. Eisenfeld's memory was less retentive. When he came home a few nights later, he had completely forgotten the fleeting squirm of uneasiness which the reference to the Saint in the *Elmford News* had given him. He had almost as completely forgotten his late Police Commissioner; although when he did remember him, it was with a feeling of pleasant satisfaction that he had been so easily got rid of. Already he had selected another occupant for that conveniently vacated office, who he was assured would prove more amenable to reason. And that night he was expecting another visitor whose mission would give him an almost equal satisfaction.

The visitor arrived punctually, and was hospitably received with a highball and a cigar. After a brief exchange of cordial commonplaces, the visitor produced a bulging wallet and slid it casually across the table. In the same casual manner Mr. Eisenfeld picked it up, inspected the contents and slipped it into his pocket. After which the two men refilled their glasses and smoked for a while in companionable silence.

"We got the last of that cement delivered yesterday," remarked the visitor, in the same way that he might have bridged a conversational hiatus with some bromidic comment on the weather.

Mr. Eisenfeld nodded.

"Yeah, I saw it. They got the monument about one quarter full already—I was by there this afternoon."

Mr. Schmidt gazed vacantly at the ceiling.

"Any time you've got any other job like that, we'll still be making good cement," he said, with the same studied casualness. "You know we always like to look after anyone who can put a bit of business our way."

"Sure, I'll remember it," said Mr. Eisenfeld amiably.

Mr. Schmidt fingered his chin. "Too bad about Provost, wasn't it?" he remarked.

"Yeah," agreed Mr. Eisenfeld, "too bad."

Half an hour later he escorted his guest out to his car. The light over the porch had gone out when he returned to the house, and without giving it any serious thought he attributed the failure to a blown fuse or a faulty bulb. He was in too good a humour to be annoyed by it; and he was actually humming complacently to himself as he groped his way up the dark steps. The light in the hall had gone out as well, and he frowned faintly over the idle deduction that it must have been a fuse. He pushed through the door and turned to close it; and then a hand clamped over his mouth, and something hard and uncongenial pressed into the small of his back. A gentle voice spoke chillingly in his ear.

"Just one word"—it whispered invitingly—"just one word out of you, Al, and your life is going to be even shorter than I expected.

Mr. Eisenfeld stood still, with his muscles rigid. He was not a physical coward but the grip which held his head pressed back against the chest of the unknown man behind him had a firm competence which announced that there were adequate sinews behind it to back up its persuasion in any hand-to-hand struggle. Also, the object which prodded into the middle of his spine constituted an argument in itself which he was wise enough to understand.

The clasp on his mouth relaxed tentatively and slid down to rest lightly on his throat. The same gentle voice breathed again on his right eardrum.

"Let us go out into the great open spaces and look at the night," said the Saint.

Mr. Eisenfeld allowed himself to be conducted back down the walk over which he had just returned. He had very little choice in the matter. The gun of the uninvited guest remained glued to his backbone as if it intended to take root there, and he knew that the fingers which rested so caressingly on his windpipe would have detected the first shout he tried to utter before it could reach his vocal cords.

A few yards down the road a car waited with its lights burning. They stopped beside it.

"Open the door and get in."

Mr. Eisenfeld obeyed. The gun slipped round from his back to his left side as his escort followed him into the seat behind the wheel. Simon started the engine and reached over to slip the gear lever into first. The headlights were switched on as they moved away from the curb; and Mr. Eisenfeld found his first opportunity of giving vent to the emotions that were chasing themselves through his system.

"What the hell's the idea of this?" he demanded violently.

"We're going for a little drive, dear old bird," answered the Saint. "But I promise you won't have to walk home. My intentions are more honourable than anyone like you could easily imagine."

"If you're trying to kidnap me," Eisenfeld blustered, "I'm telling you you can't get away with it. I'll see that you get what's coming to you! Why you . . ."

Simon let him make his speech without interruption. The lights of the residential section twinkled steadily past them, and presently even Eisenfeld's flood of outraged eloquence dwindled away before that impenetrable calm. They drove on over the practically deserted roads—it was after midnight, and there were very few attractions in that area to induce the pious citizens of Elmford to lose their beauty sleep—and presently Mr. Eisenfeld realized that their route would take them past the site of the almost completed Elmford Riviera on the bank of the river above the town.

He was right in his deduction, except for the word "past." As a matter of fact, the car jolted off the main highway onto the unfinished road which lead down to Elmford's playground; and exactly in the middle of the two-mile esplanade, under the very shadow of the central monument which Sam Purdell had been so modestly unwilling to accept, it stopped.

"This is as far as we go," said the Saint, and motioned politely to the door.

Mr. Eisenfeld got out. He was sweating a little with perfectly natural fear, and above that there was a growing cloud of mystification through which he was trying to discover some coherent design in the extraordinary series of events which had enveloped him in those last few minutes. He seemed to be caught up in the machinery of some hideous nightmare, in which the horror was intensified by the fact that he could find no reason in the way it moved. If he was indeed the victim of an attempt at kidnapping, he couldn't understand why he should have been brought to a place like that; but just then there was no other explanation that he could see.

The spidery lines of scaffolding on the monument rose up in a futuristic filigree over his head, and at the top of it the shadowy outlines of the chute where the cement was mixed and poured into the hollow mould of stone roosted like a grotesque and angular prehistoric bird.

"Now we'll climb up and look at the view," said the Saint.

Still wondering, Mr. Eisenfeld felt himself steered towards a ladder which ran up one side of the scaffolding. He climbed mechanically, as he was ordered, while a stream of unanswerable questions drummed bewilderingly through his brain. Once the wild idea came to him to kick downwards at the head of the man who followed him; but when he looked down he saw that the head was several rungs below his feet, keeping a safely measured distance, and when he stopped climbing, the man behind him stopped also. Eisenfeld went on, up through the dark. He could have shouted then, but he knew that he was a mile or more from the nearest person who might have heard him.

They came out on the plank staging which ran around the top of the monument. A moment later, as he looked back, he saw the silhouette of his unaccountable kidnapper rising up against the dimly luminous background of stars and reaching the platform to lean lazily against one of the ragged ends of scaffold pole which rose above the narrow catwalk. Behind him, the hollow shaft of the mon-

ument was a square void of deeper blackness in the
surrounding dark.

"This is the end of your journey, Al," said the
stranger softly. "But before you go, there are just
one or two things I'd like to remind you about.
Also, we haven't been properly introduced, which
is probably making things rather difficult for you.
You had better know me . . . I am the Saint."

Eisenfeld started and almost overbalanced.
Where had he heard that name before? Suddenly
he remembered, and an uncanny chill crawled over
his flesh.

"There are various reasons why it doesn't seem
necessary for you to go on living," went on that
very gentle and dispassionate voice, "and your ugly
face is only one of them. This is a pretty cockeyed
world when you take it all round, but people like
you don't improve it. Also, I have heard a story
from a girl called Molly Provost—her father was
Police Commissioner until Tuesday night, I believe."

"She's a liar," gasped Eisenfeld hoarsely.
"You're crazy! Listen—"

He would have sworn that the stranger had never touched him except with his gun since they got
into the car, but suddenly an electric flashlight
spilled a tiny strip of luminance over the boards
between them, and in the bright centre of the beam
he saw the other's hand running through the contents of a wallet which looked somehow familiar.
All at once Eisenfeld recognized it and clutched un-
believingly at his pocket. The wallet which his
guest had given him an hour ago was gone; and
Eisenfeld's heart almost stopped beating.

"What are you doing with that?" he croaked.

"Just seeing how much this installment of graft

is worth," answered the Saint calmly. "And it looks exactly like thirty thousand dollars to me. Well, it might have been more, but I suppose it will have to do. I promised Molly that I'd see she was looked after, but I don't see why it shouldn't be at your expense. Part of this is your commission for getting this cenotaph filled with cement, isn't it . . . ? It seems very appropriate."

Eisenfeld's throat constricted, and the blood began to pound in his temples.

"I'll get you for this," he snarled. "You lousy crook."

"Maybe I am a crook," said the Saint, in a voice that was no more than a breath of sound in the still night. "But in between times I'm something more. In my simple way I am a kind of justice. . . . Do you know any good reason why you should wait any longer for what you deserve?"

There is a time in every man's life when he knows beyond doubt or common fear that the threads of destiny are running out. It had happened to Al Eisenfeld too suddenly for him to understand—he had no time to look back and count the incredible minutes in which his world had been turned upside down. Perhaps he himself had no clear idea what he was doing, but he knew that he was hearing death in the quiet voice that spoke out of the darkness in front of him.

His muscles carried him away without any conscious command from his brain, and he was unaware of the queer growling cry that rattled in his throat. There was a crash of sound in front of him as he sprang blindly forward, and a tongue of reddish-orange flame spat out of the darkness almost in his face. . . .

Simon Templar steadied himself on one of the

scaffold poles and stared down into the square black mould of the monument; but there was nothing that he could see, and the silence was unbroken. After a while his fingers let go the gun, and a couple of seconds later the thud of its burying itself in the wet cement at the bottom of the shaft echoed hollowly back to him.

Presently he climbed up to the chute from which the monument was being filled. He found a great mound of sacks of cement stacked beside it ready for use, and, after a little more search, a hose conveniently arranged to provide water. He was busy for three hours before he decided that he had done enough.

"And knowing that these thoughts are beating in all our hearts," boomed the voice of the Distinguished Personage through eight loud-speakers, "it will always be my proudest memory that I was deemed worthy of the honour of unveiling this eternal testimonial to the man who has devoted his life to the task of making the people of Elmford proud and happy in their great city—the mayor whom you all know and love so well, Sam Purdell!"

The flag which covered the carved inscription on the base of the Purdell memorial fluttered down. A burst of well-organized cheering volleyed from five thousand throats. The cameramen dashed forward with clicking shutters. The bandmaster raised his baton. The brass and wood winds inflated their lungs. A small urchin close to the platform swallowed a piece of chewing gum, choked, and began to cry. . . .The strains of the "Star Spangled Banner" blasted throbbingly through the afternoon air.

Then, to the accompaniment of a fresh howl of cheering, Sam Purdell stepped to the microphone. He wiped his eyes and swallowed once or twice before he spoke.

"My friends," he said, "this is not a time when I would ask you to listen to a speech. There ain't—isn't anything I can think of worthy of this honour you have done me. I can only repeat the promise which you have all heard me make before—that while I am Mayor of this city there will be only one principle in everything over which I have control: Honesty and a square deal for every man, woman and child in Elmford."

The cheers followed his car as he drove away accompanied by his round perspiring wife and his round perspiring daughters. Mrs. Purdell clutched his hand in a warm moist grip.

"That was such a beautiful speech you made, Sam," she said a little tearfully.

Sam Purdell shook his head. He had one secret sorrow.

"I wish Al could have been there," he said.

IV THE WICKED COUSIN

WHEN SIMON TEMPLAR arrived in Los Angeles there
was a leaden ceiling of cloud over the sky and a
cool wind blowing. A few drops of unenthusiastic
rain moistened the pavements and speckled the
shoulders of his coat. The porter who was loading
his bags into a taxi assured him that it was most
unusual weather, and he felt instantly at home.

Later on, comfortably stretched out on a divan
in the sitting room of his suite at the hotel in Hollywood upon which he had chosen to confer the
somewhat debatable honour of his tenancy, with a
highball at his elbow and a freshly lighted cigarette
smouldering contently between his lips, he turned
the pages of the address book on his knee and considered what his next steps should be to improve
that first feeling of a welcome return.

He was not there on business. To be quite accurate, none of the stages of the last few months of
carefree wandering which had just completed their
vague object of leading him across America from
coast to coast had been undertaken with a view to
business. If business had materialized on more
than one occasion, it was because there was something about Simon Templar which attracted adven-

ture by the same kind of mysterious but in-
escapable cosmic law which compels a magnet to
attract steel or a politician to attract attention; and
if much of that business was not looked upon
favourably by the Law—or would not have been
favourably looked upon if the Law had known all
that there was to know about it—this was because
Simon Templar's business had an unfortunate habit of falling into categories which gave many people
good reason to wonder what right he had to the
nickname of the Saint by which he was far more
widely known than he was by his baptismal titles.
It is true that these buccaneering raids of his which
had earned him the subtitle of "The Robin Hood
of Modern Crime" were invariably undertaken
against the property, and occasionally the persons,
of citizens who by no stretch of the imagination
could have been called desirable; but the Law took
no official cognizance of such small details. The
Law, in the Saint's opinion, was a stodgy and
elephantine institution which was chiefly justified
in its existence by the pleasantly musical explosive
noises which it made when he broke it.

Certainly he was not thinking of business. In
Hollywood he had many genuine friends, few of
whom gave much consideration to the sensational
legends that were associated with his name in less
unsophisticated circles, and his only immediate
problem was to which one of them he should first
break the dazzling news of his arrival. He paused at
one name after another, recalling its personality:
movie executives, directors, writers, actors and
actresses both great and small and a certain
number of ordinary human beings. He wanted—
what did he want? A touch of excitement, prefera-

bly feminine, beauty, a little of the glamour and gay unreality with which the very name of Hollywood is inseparably linked in imagination if not in fact. He wanted some of these things very much. His last stop had been made in the state of Utah.

There was a girl called Jacqueline Laine whom Simon remembered suddenly, as one does sometimes remember people, with a sense of startling familiarity and a kind of guilty amazement that he should have allowed her to slip out of his mind for so long. Once she was remembered, he had no more hesitation. No one else could have been so obviously the one person in the world whom he had to call up at that moment.

He picked up the telephone.

"Hello, Jacqueline," he said when she answered. "Do you know who this is?"

"I know," she said. "It's Franklin D. Roosevelt."

"You have a marvellous memory. Do you still eat?"

"Whenever I'm thirsty. Do you?"

"I nibble a crumb now and then. Come out with me tonight and see if we can still take it."

"Simon, I'd love to; but I'm in the most frantic muddle—"

"So is the rest of the world, darling. But it's two years since I've seen you, and that's about seven hundred and thirty days too long. Don't you realize that I've come halfway around the world, surviving all manner of perils and slaying large numbers of ferocious dragons, just to get here in time to take you out to dinner tonight?"

"I know, but— Oh well. It would be so thrilling to see you. Come around about seven and I'll try to get a bit straightened out before then."

"I'll be there," said the Saint.

He spent some of the intervening time in making himself the owner of a car, and shortly after half-past six he turned it westwards into the stream of studio traffic homing towards Beverly Hills. Some-where along Sunset Boulevard he turned off to the right and began to climb one of the winding roads that led up into the hills. The street lights were just beginning to trace their twinkling geometrical network over the vast panorama of cities spread out beneath him, as the car soared smoothly higher into the luminous blue-grey twilight.

He found his way with the certainty of vivid re-membrance; and he was fully ten minutes early when he pulled the car into a bay by the roadside before the gate of Jacqueline Laine's house. He climbed out and started towards the gate, lighting a cigarette as he went, and as he approached it he perceived that somebody else was approaching the same gate from the opposite side. Changing his course a little to the left so that the departing guest would have room to pass him, the Saint observed that he was a small and elderly gent arrayed in clothes so shapeless and ill fitting that they gave his figure a comical air of having been loosely and in-accurately strung together from a selection of stuffed bags of cloth. He wore a discolored Pan-ama hat of weird and wonderful architecture, and carried an incongruous green umbrella furled, but still flapping in a bedraggled and forlorn sort of way, under his left arm; his face was rubicund and bulbous like his body, looking as if it had been carelessly slapped together out of a few odd lumps of pink plasticine.

As Simon moved to the left, the elderly gent duplicated the manoeuvre. Simon turned his feet and swerved politely to the right. The elderly gent did exactly the same, as if he were Simon's own reflection in a distorting mirror. Simon stopped altogether and decided to economize energy by letting the elderly gent make the next move in the ballet on his own.

Whereupon he discovered that the game of undignified dodging in which he had just prepared to surrender his part was caused by some dimly discernible ambition of the elderly gent's to hold converse with him. Standing in front of him and blinking short-sightedly upwards from his lower altitude to the Saint's six foot two, with his mouth hanging vacantly open like an inverted "U" and three long yellow teeth hanging down like stalactites from the top, the elderly gent tapped him on the chest and said, very earnestly and distinctly: "Hig fwmgn glugl phnihklu hgrm skhlglgl?"

"I beg your pardon?" said the Saint vaguely.

"Hig fwmgn," repeated the elderly gent, "glugl phnihklu hgrm skhlglgl?"

Simon considered the point.

"If you ask me," he replied at length, "I should say sixteen."

The elderly gent's knobbly face seemed to take on a brighter shade of pink. He clutched the lapels of the Saint's coat, shaking him slightly in a positive passion of anguish.

"Flogh ghoglu sk," he pleaded, "klngnt hu ughlgstghnd?"

Simon shook his head.

"No," he said judiciously, "you're thinking of weevils."

The little man bounced about like a rubber doll. His eyes squinted with a kind of frantic despair.

"Ogmighogho," he almost screamed, "klngt hu ughglstghnd? Ik ghln ngmnpp sktlghko! Klugt hu hgr? *Ik wgnt hlg phnihkln hgrm skhlglgl!*"

The Saint sighed. He was by nature a kindly man to those whom the Gods had afflicted, but time was passing and he was thinking of Jacqueline Laine.

"I'm afraid not, dear old bird," he murmured regretfully. "There used to be one, but it died. Sorry, I'm sure."

He patted the elderly gent apologetically upon the shoulder, steered his way around him, and passed on out of earshot of the frenzied sputtering noises that continued to honk despairingly through the dusk behind him. Two minutes later he was with Jacqueline.

Jacqueline Laine was twenty-three; she was tall and slender; she had grey eyes that twinkled and a demoralizing mouth. Both of these temptations were in play as she came towards him; but he was still slightly shaken by his recent encounter.

"Have you got any more village idiots hidden around?" he asked warily, as he took her hands; and she was puzzled.

"We used to have several, but they've all got into Congress. Did you want one to take home?"

"My God, no," said the Saint fervently. "The one I met at the gate was bad enough. Is he your latest boy friend?"

Her brow cleared.

"Oh, you mean the old boy with the cleft palate? Isn't he marvellous? I think he's got a screw loose or something. He's been hanging around all day—

he keeps ringing the bell and bleating at me. I'd just sent him away for the third time. Did he try to talk to you?"

"He did sort of wag his adenoids at me," Simon admitted, "but I don't think we actually got on to common ground. I felt quite jealous of him for a bit, until I realized that he couldn't possibly kiss you nearly as well as I can, with that set of teeth."

He proceeded to demonstrate this.

"I'm still in a hopeless muddle," she said presently. "But I'll be ready in five minutes. You can be fixing a cocktail while I finish myself off."

In the living room there was an open trunk in one corner and a half-filled packing case in the middle of the floor. There were scattered heaps of paper around it, and a few partially wrapped and unidentifiable objects on the table. The room had that curiously naked and inhospitable look which a room has when it has been stripped of all those intimately personal odds and ends of junk which make it a home, and only the bare furniture is left.

The Saint raised his eyebrows.

"Hullo," he said. "Are you moving?"

"Sort of." She shrugged. "Moving out, anyway."

"Where to?"

"I don't know."

He realized then that there should have been someone else there, in that room.

"Isn't your grandmother here any more?"

She died four weeks ago."

"I'm sorry."

"She was a good soul. But she was terribly old. Do you know she was just ninety-seven?" She held his hand for a moment. "I'll tell you all about it when I come down. Do you remember where to find the bottles?"

"Templars and elephants never forget."

He blended bourbon, applejack, vermouth and bitters, skilfully and with the zeal of an artist, while he waited for her, remembering the old lady whom he had seen so often in that room. Also, he remembered the affectionate service that Jacqueline had always lavished on her, cheerfully limiting her own enjoyment of life to meet the demands of an unconscious tyrant who would allow no one else to look after her, and wondered if there was any realistic reason to regret the ending of such a long life. She had, he knew, looked after Jacqueline herself in her time, and had brought her up as her own child since she was left an orphan at the age of three; but life must always belong to the young. . . . He thought that for Jacqueline it must be a supreme escape, but he knew that she would never say so.

She came down punctually in the five minutes which she had promised. She had changed her dress and put a comb through her hair, and with that seemed to have achieved more than any other woman could have shown for an hour's fiddling in front of a mirror.

"You should have been in pictures," said the Saint, and he meant it.

"Maybe I shall," she said. "I'll have to do something to earn a living now."

"Is it as bad as that?"

She nodded.

"But I can't complain. I never had to work for anything before. Why shouldn't I start? Other people have to."

"Is that why you're moving out?"

"The house isn't mine."

"But didn't the old girl leave you anything?"

"She left me some letters."

The Saint almost spilt his drink. He sat down heavily on the edge of the table.

"She left you some *letters*? After you'd practically been a slave to her ever since you came out of finishing school? What did she do with the rest of her property—leave it to a home for stray cats?"

"No, she left it to Harry."

"Who?"

"Her grandson."

"I didn't know you had any brothers."

"I haven't. Harry Westler is my cousin. He's— well, as a matter of fact he's a sort of black sheep. He's a gambler, and he was in prison once for forging a check. Nobody else in the family would have anything to do with him, and if you believe what they used to say about him they were probably quite right; but Granny always had a soft spot for him. She never believed he could do anything wrong—he was just a mischievous boy to her. Well, you know how old she was . . ."

"And she left everything to him?"

"Practically everything. I'll show you."

She went to a drawer of the writing table and brought him a typewritten sheet. He saw that it was a copy of a will, and turned to the details of the bequests.

To my dear granddaughter Jacqueline Laine, who has taken care of me so thoughtfully and unselfishly for four years, One Hundred Dollars and my letters from Sidney Farlance, knowing that she will find them of more value than anything else I could leave her.

To my cook, Eliza Jefferson, and my chauffeur, Albert Gordon, One Hundred Dollars each, for their loyal service.

The remainder of my estate, after these deductions, including my house and other personal belongings, to my dear grandson Harry Westler, hoping that it will help him to make the success of life of which I have always believed him capable.

Simon folded the sheet and dropped it on the table from his finger tips as if it were infected.

"Suffering Judas," he said helplessly. "After all you did for her—to pension you off on the same scale as the cook and the chauffeur! And what about Harry—doesn't he propose to do anything about it?"

"Why should he? The will's perfectly clear."

"Why shouldn't he? Just because the old crow went off her rocker in the last days of senile decay is no reason why he shouldn't do something to put it right. There must have been enough for both of you."

"Not so much. They found that Granny had been living on her capital for years. There was only about twenty thousand dollars left—and the house."

"What of it? He could spare half."

Jacqueline smiled—a rather tired little smile.

"You haven't met Harry. He's—difficult . . . He's been here, of course. The agents already have his instructions to sell the house and the furniture. He gave me a week to get out, and the week is up the day after tomorrow. . . . I couldn't possibly ask him for anything."

Simon lighted a cigarette as if it tasted of bad

eggs and scowled malevolently about the room.

"The skunk! And so you get chucked out into the wide world with nothing but a hundred dollars."

"And the letters," she added ruefully.

"What the hell are these letters?"

"They're love letters," she said; and the Saint looked as if he would explode.

"Love letters?" he repeated in an awful voice.

"Yes. Granny had a great romance when she was a girl. Her parents wouldn't let her get any further with it because the boy hadn't any money and his family wasn't good enough. He went abroad with one of these heroic young ideas of making a fortune in South America and coming back in a gold-plated carriage to claim her. He died of fever somewhere in Brazil very soon after, but he wrote her three letters—two from British Guiana and one from Colombia. Oh, I know them by heart —I used to have to read them aloud to Granny almost every night, after her eyes got too bad for her to be able to read them herself. They're just the ordinary simple sort of thing that you'd expect in the circumstances, but to Granny they were the most precious thing she had. I suppose she had some funny old idea in her head that they'd be just as precious to me."

"She must have been screwy," said the Saint.

Jacqueline came up and put a hand over his mouth. "She was very good to me when I was a kid," she said.

"I know, but—" Simon flung up his arms hopelessly. And then, almost reluctantly, he began to laugh. "But it does mean that I've just come back in time. And we'll have so much fun tonight that you won't even think about it for a minute."

Probably he made good his boast, for Simon Templar brought to the solemn business of enjoying himself the same gay zest and inspired impetuosity which he brought to his battles with the technicalities of the law. But if he made her forget, he himself remembered; and when he followed her into the living room of the house again much later, for a good night drink, the desolate scene of interrupted packing, and the copy of the will still lying on the table where he had put it down, brought the thoughts with which he had been subconsciously playing throughout the evening back into the forefront of his mind.

"Are you going to let Harry get away with it?" he asked her, with a sudden characteristic directness.

The girl shrugged.

"What else can I do?"

"I have an idea," said the Saint; and his blue eyes danced with an unholy delight which she had never seen in them before.

Mr. Westler was not a man whose contacts with the Law had conspired to make him particularly happy about any of its workings; and therefore when he saw that the card which was brought to him in his hotel bore in its bottom left-hand corner the name of a firm with the words "Attorneys at Law" underneath it, he suffered an immediate hollow twinge in the base of his stomach for which he could scarcely be blamed. A moment's reflection, however, reminded him that another card with a similar inscription had recently been the forerunner of an extremely welcome windfall, and with this reassuring thought he told the bellboy to

·bring the visitor into his presence.

Mr. Tombs, of Tombs, Tombs, and Tombs, as the card introduced him, was a tall lean man with neatly brushed white hair, bushy white eyebrows, a pair of gold-rimmed and drooping pince-nez on the end of a broad black ribbon and an engagingly avuncular manner which rapidly completed the task of restoring Harry Westler's momentarily shaken confidence. He came to the point with professional efficiency combined with professional pomposity.

"I have come to see you in connection with the estate of the—ah—late Mrs. Laine. I understand that you are her heir."

"That's right," said Mr. Westler.

He was a dark, flashily dressed man with small greedy eyes and a face rather reminiscent of that of a sick horse.

"Splendid." The lawyer placed his finger tips on his knees and leant forward peering benevolently over the rims of his glasses. "Now I for my part am representing the Sesame Mining Development Corporation."

He said this more or less as if he were announcing himself as the personal herald of Jehovah, but Mr. Westler's mind ran in practical channels.

"Did my grandmother have shares in the company?" he asked quickly.

"Ah—ah—no. That is—ah—no. Not exactly. But I understand that she was in possession of a letter or document which my clients regard as extremely valuable."

"A letter?"

"Exactly. But perhaps I had better give you an outline of the situation. Your grandmother was in

3 her youth greatly—ah—enamoured of a certain
Sidney Farlance. Perhaps at some time or other
you have heard her speak of him."

"Yes."

"For various reasons her parents refused to give
their consent to the alliance; but the young people
for their part refused to take no for an answer, and
Farlance went abroad with the intention of making
his fortune in foreign parts and returning in due
course to claim his bride. In this ambition he was
unhappily frustrated by his—ah—premature de-
cease in Brazil. But it appears that during his
travels in British Guiana he did become the owner
of a mining concession in a certain very inac-
cessible area of territory. British Guiana, as you
are doubtless aware," continued Mr. Tombs in his
dry pedagogic voice, "is traditionally reputed to be
the source of the legend of El Dorado, the Gilded
King, who was said to cover himself with pure gold
and to wash it from him in the waters of a sacred
lake called Manoa—"

"Never mind all that baloney," said Harry
Westler, who was not interested in history or
mythology. "Tell me about this concession."

Mr. Tombs pressed his lips with a pained expression but he went on.

"At the time it did not appear that gold could be
profitably obtained from this district and the claim
was abandoned and forgotten. Modern engineering methods, however, have recently revealed de-
posits of almost fabulous value in the district, and
my clients have obtained a concession to work it
over a very large area of ground. Subsequent inves-
tigations into their title, meanwhile, have brought
out the existence of this small—ah—prior con-

cession granted to Sidney Farlance, which is situated almost in the centre of my client's territory and in a position which—ah—exploratory drillings have shown to be one of the richest areas in the district."

Mr. Westler digested the information, and in place of the first sinking vacuum which had afflicted his stomach when he saw the word Law on his visitor's card, a sudden and ecstatic awe localized itself in the same place and began to cramp his lungs as if he had accidentally swallowed a rubber balloon with his breakfast and it was being rapidly inflated by some supernatural agency.

"You mean my grandmother owned this concession?"

"That is what—ah—my clients are endeavouring to discover. Farlance himself, of course, left no heirs, and we have been unable to trace any surviving members of his family. In the course of our inquiries, however, we did learn of his—ah—romantic interest in your grandmother, and we have every reason to believe that in the circumstances he would naturally have made her the beneficiary of any such asset, however problematical its value may have seemed at the time."

"And you want to buy it out—is that it?"

"Ah—yes. That is—ah—provided that our deductions are correct and the title can be established. I may say that my clients would be prepared to pay very liberally—"

"They'd have to," said Mr. Westler briskly. "How much are they good for?"

The lawyer raised his hands deprecatingly.

"You need have no alarm, my dear Mr. Westler. The actual figure would, of course, be a matter for negotiation but it would doubtless run into a number of millions. But first of all, you understand, we must trace the actual concession papers which will be sufficient to establish your right to negotiate. Now it seems that in view of the relationship between Farlance and your grandmother, she would probably have treasured his letters as women do even though she later married someone else, particularly if there was a document of that sort among them. People don't usually throw things like that away. In that case you will doubtless have inherited these letters along with her other personal property. Possibly you have not yet had an occasion to peruse them, but if you would do so as soon as possible—"

One of Harry Westler's few Napoleonic qualities was a remarkable capacity for quick and constructive thinking.

"Certainly I have the letters," he said, "but I haven't gone through them yet. My lawyer has them at present and he's in San Francisco today. He'll be back tomorrow morning, and I'll get hold of them at once. Come and see me again tomorrow afternoon and I expect I'll have some news for you."

"Tomorrow afternoon, Mr. Westler? Certainly. I think that will be convenient. Ah—certainly." The lawyer stood up, took off his pince-nez, polished them and revolved them like a windmill on the end of their ribbon. "This has indeed been a most happy meeting, my dear sir. And may I say that I hope that tomorrow afternoon it will be even happier?"

"You can go on saying that right up till the time we start talking prices," said Harry.

The door had scarcely closed behind Mr. Tombs when he was on the telephone to his cousin. He suppressed a sigh of relief when he heard her voice and announced as casually as he could his intention of coming around to see her.

"I think we ought to have another talk—I was terribly upset by the shock of Granny's death when I saw you the other day and I'm afraid I wasn't quite myself, but I'll make all the apologies you like when I get there," he said in an unfamiliarly gentle voice which cost him a great effort to achieve, and was grabbing his hat before the telephone was properly back on its bracket.

He made a call at the bank on his way, and sat in the taxi which carried him up into the hills as if its cushions had been upholstered with hot spikes. The exact words of that portion of the will which referred to the letters drummed through his memory with a staggering significance. *"My letters from Sidney Farlance, knowing that she will find them of more value than anything else I could leave her."* The visit of Mr. Tombs had made him understand them perfectly. His grandmother had known what was in them; but did Jacqueline know? His heart almost stopped beating with anxiety.

As he leapt out of the taxi and dashed towards the house he cannoned into a small and weirdly apparelled elderly gent who was apparently emerging from the gate at the same time. Mr. Westler checked himself involuntarily, and the elderly gent, sent flying by the impact, bounced off a gatepost and tottered back at him. He clutched Harry by the sleeve and peered up at him pathetically.

"Glhwf hngwglgl," he said pleadingly, "kngnduk glu bwtlhjp mnyihgli?"

"Oh, go climb a tree," snarled Mr. Westler impatiently.

He pushed the little man roughly aside and went on.

Jacqueline opened the door to him, and Mr. Westler steeled himself to kiss her on the forehead with cousinly affection.

"I was an awful swine the other day, Jackie. I don't know what could have been the matter with me. I've always been terribly selfish," he said with an effort, "and at the time I didn't really see how badly Granny had treated you. She didn't leave you anything except those letters, did she?"

"She left me a hundred dollars," said Jacqueline calmly.

"A hundred dollars!" said Harry indignantly. "After you'd given up everything else to take care of her. And she left me more than twenty thousand dollars and the house and everything else in it. It's —disgusting! But I don't have to take advantage of it, do I? I've been thinking a lot about it lately—"

Jacqueline lighted a cigarette and regarded him stonily.

"Thanks," she said briefly. "But I haven't asked you for any charity."

"It isn't charity," protested Mr. Westler virtuously. "It's just a matter of doing the decent thing. The lawyers have done their share—handed everything over to me and seen that the will was carried out. Now we can start again. We could pool everything again and divide it the way we think it ought to be divided."

"As far as I'm concerned, that's been done already."

"But I'm not happy about it. I've got all the

money, and you know what I'm like. I'll probably gamble it all away in a few months."

"That's your affair."

"Oh, don't be like that, Jackie. I've apologized, haven't I? Besides, what Granny left you is worth a lot more than money. I mean those letters of hers. I'd willingly give up five thousand dollars of my share if I could have had those. They're the one thing of the old lady's which really means a great deal to me."

"You're becoming very sentimental all of a sudden, aren't you?" asked the girl curiously.

"Maybe I am. I suppose you can't really believe that a rotter like me could feel that way about anything, but Granny was the only person in the world who ever really believed any good of me and liked me in spite of everything. If I gave you five thousand dollars for those letters, it wouldn't be charity —I'd be paying less than I think they're worth. Let's put it that way if you'd rather, Jackie. An ordinary business deal. If I had them," said Mr. Westler, with something like a sob in his voice, "they'd always be a reminder to me of the old lady and how good she was. They might help me to go straight . . ."

His emotion was so touching that even Jacqueline's cynical incredulity lost some of its assurance. Harry Westler was playing his part with every technical trick that he knew, and he had a mastery of these emotional devices which victims far more hard-boiled than Jacqueline had experienced to their cost.

"I'm thoroughly ashamed of myself and I want to put things right in any way I can. Don't make me feel any worse than I do already. Look here, I'll give you ten thousand dollars for the letters and I won't regret a penny of it. You won't regret it either, will you, if they help me to keep out of trouble in future?"

Jacqueline smiled in spite of herself. It was not in her nature to bear malice, and it was very hard for her to resist an appeal that was made in those terms. Also, with the practical side of her mind, she was honest enough to realize that her grandmother's letters had no sentimental value for her whatever, and that ten thousand dollars was a sum of money which she could not afford to refuse unless her pride was compelled to forbid it; her night out with the Saint had helped her to forget her problems for the moment, but she had awakened that morning with a very sober realization of the position in which she was going to find herself within the next forty-eight hours.

"If you put it like that I can't very well refuse, can I?" she said, and Harry jumped up and clasped her fervently by the hand.

"You'll really do it, Jackie? You don't know how much I appreciate it."

She disengaged herself quietly.

"It doesn't do me any harm," she told him truthfully. "Would you like to have the letters now?"

"If they're anywhere handy. I brought some money along with me, so we can fix it all up right away."

She went upstairs and fetched the letters from the dressing table in her grandmother's room. Mr. Westler took them and tore off the faded ribbon with which they were tied together with slightly trembling fingers which she attributed to an unexpected depth of emotion. One by one he took them out of their envelopes and read rapidly through them. The last sheet of the third letter was a different kind of paper from the rest. The paper was brown and discoloured and cracked in the folds, and the ink had the rust-brown hue of great age; but he saw the heavy official seal in one corner and strained his eyes to decipher the stiff old-fashioned script.

We, Philip Edmond Wodehouse, Commander of the Most Noble Order of the Bath Governor in the name of His Britannic Majesty of the Colony of British Guiana, by virtue of the powers conferred upon us by His Majesty's Privy Council, do hereby proclaim and declare to all whom it may concern that we have this day granted to Sidney Farlance, a subject of His Majesty the King, and to his heirs and assigns being determined by the possession of this authority, the sole right to prospect and mine for minerals of any kind whatsoever in the territory indicated and described in the sketch map at the foot of this authority, for the term of nine hundred and ninety-nine years from the date of these presents.

Given under our hand and seal this third day of January Eighteen Hundred and Fifty-Six.

At the bottom of the sheet below the map and description was scrawled in a different hand: "*This is all for you. S.F.*"

Harry Westler stuffed the letters into his pocket and took out his wallet. His heart was beating in a delirious rhythm of ecstasy and sending the blood roaring through his ears like the crashing crescendo of a symphony. The Gates of Paradise seemed to have opened up and deluged him with all their reservoirs of bliss. The whole world was his sweet-

heart. If the elderly gent whose strange nasal gar-
glings he had dismissed so discourteously a short
time ago had cannoned into him again at that moment, it is almost certain that Mr. Westler would
not have told him to go and climb a tree. He would
probably have kissed him on both cheeks and given
him a nickel.

For the first time in his life, Harry Westler
counted out ten thousand-dollar bills as cheerfully
as he would have counted them in.

"There you are, Jackie. And I'm not kidding—it
takes a load off my mind. If you think of anything
else I can do for you, just let me know."

"I think you've done more than anyone could
have asked," she said generously. "Won't you stay
and have a drink?"

Mr. Westler declined the offer firmly. He had no
moral prejudice against drinking, and in fact he
wanted a drink very badly, but more particularly
he wanted to have it in a place where he would not
have to place any more restraint on the shouting
rhapsodies that were seething through his system
like bubbles through champagne.

Some two hours later, when Simon Templar
drifted into the house, he found Jacqueline still
looking slightly dazed. She flung her arms around
his neck and kissed him.

"Simon!" she gasped. "You must be a mascot or
something. You'll never guess what's happened."

"I'll tell you exactly what's happened," said the
Saint calmly. "Cousin Harry has been here, told
you that he'd rather have dear old Granny's love
letters than all the money in the world and paid
you a hell of a good price for them. At least I hope
he paid you a hell of a good price."

Jacqueline gaped at him weakly.

"He paid me ten thousand dollars. But how on earth did you know? Why did he do it?"

"He did it because a lawyer called on him this morning and told him that Sidney Farlance had collared an absolutely priceless mining concession when he was in British Guiana, and that there was probably something about it in the letters which would be worth millions to whoever had them to prove his claim."

She looked at him aghast.

"A mining concession? I don't remember anything about it—"

"You wouldn't," said the Saint kindly. "It wasn't there until I slipped it in when I got you to show me the letters at breakfast time this morning. I sat up for the other half of the night faking the best imitation I could of what I thought a concession ought to look like, and apparently it was good enough for Harry. Of course I was the lawyer who told him all about it, and I think I fed him the oil pretty smoothly, so perhaps there was some excuse for him. I take it that he was quite excited about it—I see he didn't even bother to take the envelopes."

Jacqueline opened her mouth again, but what she was going to say with it remained a permanently unsolved question, for at that moment the unnecessarily vigorous ringing of a bell stopped her short. The Saint cocked his ears speculatively at the sound and a rather pleased and seraphic smile worked itself into his face.

"I expect this is Harry coming back," he said. "He wasn't supposed to see me again until tomorrow but I suppose he couldn't wait. He's probably tried to ring me up at the address I had printed on my card and discovered that there ain't no such lawyers as I was supposed to represent. It will be rather interesting to hear what he has to say."

For once, however, Simon's guess was wrong. Instead of the indignant equine features of Harry Westler, he confronted the pink imploring features of the small and shapeless elderly gent with whom he had danced prettily around the gateposts the day before. The little man's face lighted up and he bounced over the doorstep and seized the Saint joyfully by both lapels of his coat.

"Mnyng hlfwgl!" he crowed triumphantly. "Ahkgmp glglgl hndiuphwmp!"

Simon recoiled slightly.

"Yes. I know," he said soothingly. "But it's five o'clock on Fridays. Two dollars every other yard."

"Ogh hmbals!" said the little man.

He let go the Saint's coat, ducked under his arms and scuttled on into the living room.

"Oi!" said the Saint feebly.

"May I explain, sir?"

Another voice spoke from the doorway, and Simon perceived that the little man had not come alone. Someone else had taken his place on the threshold—a thin and mournful-looking individual whom the Saint somewhat pardonably took to be the little man's keeper.

"Are you looking after that?" he inquired resignedly. "And why don't you keep it on a lead?"

The mournful-looking individual shook his head.

"That is Mr. Horatio Ive, sir—he is a very rich man, but he suffers from an unfortunate impediment in his speech. Very few people can understand him. I go about with him as his interpreter, but I have been in bed for the last three days with a chill—"

A shrill war whoop from the other room interrupted the explanation.

"We'd better go and see how he's getting on," said the Saint.

"Mr. Ive is very impulsive, sir," went on the sad-looking interpreter. "He was most anxious to see somebody here, and even though I was unable to accompany him he has called here several times alone. I understand that he found it impossible to make himself understood. He practically dragged me out of bed to come with him now."

"What's he so excited about?" asked the Saint, as they walked towards the living room.

"He's interested in some letters, sir, belonging to the late Mrs. Laine. She happened to show them to him when they met once several years ago, and he wanted to buy them. She refused to sell them for sentimental reasons, but as soon as he read of her death he decided to approach her heirs."

"Are you talking about her love letters from a bird called Sidney Farlance?" Simon asked hollowly.

"Yes sir. The gentleman who worked in British Guiana. Mr. Ive is prepared to pay something like fifty thousand dollars—Is anything the matter, sir?"

Simon Templar swallowed.

"Oh, nothing," he said faintly. "Nothing at all."

They entered the living room to interrupt a scene of considerable excitement. Backing towards the wall, with a blank expression of alarm widening her eyes, Jacqueline Laine was staring dumbly at the small elderly gent, who was capering about in front of her like a frenzied redskin, spluttering yard after yard of his incomprehensible adenoidal honks interspersed with wild piercing squeaks apparently expressive of intolerable joy. In each hand he held an envelope aloft like a banner.

As his interpreter came in, he turned and rushed towards him, loosing off a fresh stream of noises like those of a hysterical duck.

"Mr. Ive is saying, sir," explained the interpreter, raising his voice harmoniously above the din, "that each of those envelopes bears a perfect example of the British Guiana one-cent magenta stamp of 1856, of which only one specimen was previously believed to exist. Mr. Ive is an ardent philatelist, sir, and these envelopes—"

Simon Templar blinked hazily at the small crudely printed stamp in the corner of the envelope which the little man was waving under his nose.

"Yes sir."

"Not the letters themselves?"

"Not the letters."

"And he's been flapping around the house all this time trying to tell somebody about it?"

"Yes sir."

Simon Templar drew a deep breath. The foundations of the world were spinning giddily around his ears but his natural resilience was unconquerable. He took out a handkerchief and mopped his brow.

"In that case," he said contentedly, "I'm sure we can do business. What do you say, Jacqueline?"

Jacqueline clutched his arm and nodded breathlessly.

"Hlgagtsk sweghlemlgl," beamed Mr. Ive.

V   THE BENEVOLENT BURGLARY

"DENNIS UMBER?" Simon Templar repeated vaguely. "I don't know . . . I think I read something about him in a newspaper some time ago, but I'm blowed if I can remember what it was. I can't keep track of every small-time crook in creation. What's he been doing?"

"I just thought you might know something about him," Inspector Fernack answered evasively.

He sat on the edge of a chair and mauled his fedora with big bony fists, looking almost comically like an elephantine edition of an office boy trying to put over a new excuse for taking an afternoon off. He glowered ferociously around the sunny room in which Simon was calmly continuing to eat breakfast and racked his brain for inspiration to keep the interview going.

For the truth was that Inspector John Fernack had not called on the Saint for information about Mr. Dennis Umber. Or about anybody else in the same category. He had a highly efficient Records Office at his disposal down on Centre Street, which was maintained for the sole purpose of answering questions like that. The name was simply an excuse that he had grabbed out of his head while he was on his way up in the elevator. Because there was really only one lawbreaker about whom Fernack needed to go to Simon Templar for information—and that was the Saint himself.

Not that even that was likely to be very profitable, either, but Fernack couldn't help it. He made the pilgrimage in the same spirit as a man who had lived under the shadow of a volcano that had been quiescent for some time might climb up to peep into the crater, with the fond hope that it might be good enough to tell him when and how it next intended to erupt. He knew he was only making a fool of himself, but that was only part of the cross he had to bear. There were times when, however hard he tried to master them, the thoughts of all the lawless mischief which that tireless buccaneer might be cooking up in secret filled his mind with such horrific nightmares that he had to do something about them or explode. The trouble was that the only thing he could think of doing was to go and have another look at the Saint in person, as if he hoped that he would be lucky enough to arrive at the very moment when Simon had decided to write out his plans on a large board and wear them hung round his neck. The knowledge of his own futility raised Fernack's blood pressure to a point that actively endangered his health; but he could no more have kept himself away from the Saint's apartment, when one of those fits of morbid uneasiness seized him, than he could have danced in a ballet.

He stuck a cigar into his mouth and bit on it with massive violence, knowing perfectly well that the Saint knew exactly what was the matter with him, and that the Saint was probably trying politely not to laugh out loud. His smouldering eyes swivelled back to the Saint with belligerent defiance. If he caught so much as the shadow of a grin on that infernally handsome face . . .

But the Saint wasn't grinning. He wasn't paying any particular attention to Fernack at all. He was reading his newspaper again, and Fernack heard him murmur: "Well, isn't that interesting?"

"Isn't what interesting?" growled the detective aggressively.

Simon folded the sheet.

"I see that the public is invited to an exhibition of Mr. Elliot Vascoe's art treasures at Mr. Vascoe's house on Knickerbocker Place. Admission will be five dollars, and all the proceeds will go to charity. The exhibition will be opened by Princess Eunice of Greece."

Fernack stiffened. He had the dizzy sense of un-reality that would overwhelm a man who had been daydreaming about what he would do if his uncle suddenly died and left him a million dollars, if a man walked straight into his office and said, "Your uncle has died and left you a million dollars."

"Were you thinking of taking over any of those art treasures?" he inquired menacingly. "Because if you were—"

"I've often thought about it," said the Saint shamelessly. "I think it's a crime for Vascoe to have so many of them. He doesn't know any more about art than a cow in a field, but he's got enough dough to buy anything his advisers tell him is worth buying and it gives him something to swank about. It would be an act of virtue to take over his collection, but I suppose you wouldn't see it that way."

Fernack's brow blackened. He could hardly believe his ears, and if he had stopped to think he wouldn't have believed them. He didn't stop.

"You're damn right I wouldn't!" he roared. "Now get this, Saint. You can get away with just so much of your line in this town, and no more. You're going to leave Vascoe's exhibition alone, or by God—"

"Of course I'm going to leave it alone," said the Saint mildly. "My paths are the paths of righteousness, and my ways are the ways of peace. You know me, Fernack. Vascoe will get what's coming to him in due time, but who am I to take it upon myself to dish it out?"

"You said—"

"I said that I'd often thought about taking over some of his art treasures. But is it a crime to think? If it was, there'd be more criminals than you could build jails for. Pass the marmalade. And try not to look so disappointed." The mockery in Simon's blue eyes was bright enough now for even Fernack to realize that the Saint was deliberately taking him over the jumps once again. "Anyone might think you wanted me to turn into a crook—and is that the right attitude for a policeman to have?"

Between Simon Templar and Mr. Elliot Vascoe, millionaire and self-styled art connoisseur, no love at all was lost. Simon disliked Vascoe on principle because he disliked all fat loudmouthed parvenus who took care to obtain great publicity for their charitable works while they practised all kinds of small meannesses on their employees. Vascoe hated the Saint because Simon had once happened to witness a motor accident in which Vascoe was driving and a child was injured and Vascoe had made the mistake of offering Simon five hundred dollars to forget what he had seen. That grievous error had not only failed to save Mr. Vascoe a penny of the fines and damages which he was subsequently compelled to pay, but it had earned him a punch on the nose which he need not otherwise have suffered.

Vascoe had made his money quickly, and the curse of the *nouveau rich* had fallen upon him. Himself debarred for ever from the possibility of being a gentleman, either by birth or breeding or native temperament, he had made up for it by carrying snobbery to new and rarely equalled highs. Besides works of art, he collected titles; for high-sounding names, and all the more obvious trappings of nobility, he had an almost fawning adoration. Therefore he provided lavish entertainment for any undiscriminating notables whom he could lure into his house with the attractions of his Parisian chef and his very excellent wine cellar, and contrived to get his name bracketed with those who were more discriminating by angling for them with the bait of charity, which it was difficult for them to refuse.

In a great many ways, Mr. Elliot Vascoe was the type of man whose excessive wealth would have been a natural target for one of the Saint's raids on those undesirable citizens whom he included in the comprehensive and descriptive classifications of "the ungodly"; but the truth is that up till then the Saint had never been interested enough to do anything about it. There were many other undesirable citizens whose unpleasantness was no less immune from the cumbersome interference of the Law, but whose villainies were on a larger scale and whose continued putrescence was a more blatant challenge to the Saint's self-appointed mission of justice. With so much egregiously inviting material lying ready to hand, it was perhaps natural that Simon should feel himself entitled to pick and choose, should tend to be what some critics might have called a trifle finicky in his selection of the specimens of ungodliness to be bopped on the bazook. He couldn't use all of them, much as he would have liked to.

But in Simon Templar's impulsive life there was a factor of Destiny that was always taking such decisions out of his hands. Anyone with a less sublime faith in his guiding star might have called it Coincidence, but to the Saint that word was merely a chicken-hearted half-truth. Certain things were ordained; and when the signs pointed there was no turning back.

Two days after Fernack's warning, he was speeding back to the city after an afternoon's swimming and basking in the sun at the Westchester Country Club when he saw a small coupe of rather ancient vintage standing by the roadside. The hood of the coupe was open, and a young man was very busy with the engine; he seemed to be considerably flustered, and from the quantity of oil on his face and forearms the success of his efforts seemed to bear no relation to the amount of energy he had put into them. Near the car stood a remarkably pretty girl, and she was what really caught the Saint's eye. She seemed distressed and frightened, twisting her hands nervously together and looking as if she was on the verge of tears.

Simon had flashed past before he realized that he knew her—he had met her at a dance some weeks before. His distaste for Mr. Elliot Vascoe did not apply to Vascoe's slim auburn-haired daughter, whom Simon would have been prepared to put forward in any company as a triumphant refutation of the theories of heredity. He jammed on his brakes and backed up to the breakdown.

"Hullo, Meryl," he said. "Is there anything I can do?"

"If you can make this Chinese washing machine go," said the young man, raising his smeared face from the bowels of the engine, "you are not only a better man than I am, but I expect you can invent linotypes in your sleep."

"This is Mr. Fulton—Mr. Templar." The girl made the introduction with breathless haste. "We've been here for three quarters of an hour . . ."

The Saint started to get out.

"I never was much of a mechanic," he murmured. "But if I can unscrew anything or screw anything up . . ."

"That wouldn't be good—Bill knows everything about cars, and he's already taken it to pieces twice." The girl's voice was shaky with dawning hope. "But if you could take me home yourself . . . I've simply *got* to be back before seven! Do you think you could do it?"

Her tone was so frantic that she made it sound like a matter of life and death.

Simon glanced at his watch and at the mileometer on the dashboard. It would be about fifteen miles to Knickerbocker Place, and it was less than twenty minutes to seven.

"I can try," he said, and turned to Fulton. "What about you—will you come on this death-defying ride?"

Fulton shook his head. He was a few years older than the girl, and Simon liked the clean-cut good looks of him.

"Don't worry about me," he said. "You try to get Meryl back. I'm going to make this prehistoric wreck move under its own steam if I stay here all night."

Meryl Vascoe was already in the Saint's car, and Simon returned to the wheel with a grin and a shrug. For a little while he was completely occupied with finding out just how high an unlawful speed he could make through the traffic on the parkway. When the Saint set out to do some fast travelling it was a hair-raising performance, but Meryl Vascoe's hair was fortunately raiseproof. She spent some minutes repairing various imperceptible details of her almost flawless face, and then she touched his knee anxiously.

"When we get there, just put me down at the corner of Sutton Place," she said. "I'll run the rest of the way. You see, if Father saw you drive up to the door he'd be sure to ask questions."

" 'What are you doing with that scoundrel?' " Simon said melodramatically. " 'Don't you know that he can't be trusted with a decent woman?' "

She laughed.

"That isn't what I'm worried about," she said. "Though I don't suppose he'd be very enthusiastic about our being together—I haven't forgotten what a scene we had about that dance where you picked me up and took me off to Harlem for the rest of the night. But the point is that I don't want him to know that I've been out driving at all."

"Why not?" asked the Saint reasonably. "The sun is shining. New York is beginning to develop its summer smell. What could you do that would be better and healthier than taking a day in the country?"

She looked at him guardedly, hesitating.

"Well—then I ought to have gone out in my own car, with one of the chauffeurs. But he'd be furious if he knew I'd been out with Bill Fulton, so when I went out this afternoon I told him I was going shopping with an old school friend."

Simon groaned.

"That old school friend—she does work long hours," he protested. "I should have thought you could have invented something better than that. However, I take it that Papa doesn't like Bill Fulton, and you do, so you meet him on the quiet. That's sensible enough. But what's your father got against him? He looked good enough to me. Doesn't he wash, or something?"

"You don't have to insult my father when I'm listening," she said stiffly; and then, in another moment, the emotions inside her overcame her loyalty. "I suppose it's because Bill isn't rich and hasn't got a title or anything . . . And then there's Lord Eastridge—"

Simon swerved the car dizzily under the arm of a policeman who was trying to hold them up.

"Who?" he demanded.

"The Earl of Eastridge—he's staying with us just now. He had to go and see some lawyers this afternoon but he'll be back for dinner; and if I'm not home and dressed when they ring the gong, Father'll have a fit."

"Poor little rich girl," said the Saint sympathetically. "So you have to dash home to play hostess to another of your father's expensive phonies."

"Oh, no; this one's perfectly genuine. He's quite nice, really, only he's so wet. But Father's been caught too often before. He got hold of this earl's passport and took it down to the British Consulate, and they said it was quite all right."

"The idea being," Simon commented shrewdly, "that Papa doesn't want any comebacks after he's made you the Countess of Eastridge."

She didn't answer at once, and Simon himself was busy with the task of passing a truck on the wrong side, whizzing over a crossing while the lights changed from amber to red and making a skidding turn under the nose of a taxi at the next red light. But there was some queer gift of humanity about him that had always had an uncanny knack of unlocking other people's conventional reserves; and besides, they had once danced together and talked much delightful nonsense while all the conventional inhabitants of Manhattan slept.

She found herself saying: "You see, all Bill's got is his radio business, and he's invented a new tube that's going to make him a fortune; but I got Father to lend him the twenty thousand dollars Bill needed to develop it. Father gave him the money but he made Bill sign a sort of mortgage that gave Father the right to take his invention away from him if the money wasn't paid back. Now Father says that if Bill tries to marry me he'll foreclose, and Bill wouldn't have anything left. I know how Bill's getting on, and I know if he only has a few months more he'll be able to pay Father back ten times over."

"Can't you wait those few months?" asked the Saint. "If Bill's on to something as good as that—"

She shook her head.

"But Father says that if I don't marry Lord Eastridge as soon as he asks me to—and I know he's going to—he'll foreclose on Bill anyway, and Bill won't get a penny for all his work." Her voice broke, and when Simon glanced at her quickly he saw the shine of tears in her eyes. "Bill doesn't know—if you tell him, I'll kill you! But he can't understand what's the matter with me. And I— I—" Her lovely face tightened with a strange bitterness. "I always thought these things only happened in pictures," she said huskily. "How can any man *be* like that?"

"You wouldn't know, darling," said the Saint gently.

That was all he said at the time, but at the same moment he resolved that he would invest five of his dollars in an admission to Mr. Elliot Vascoe's exhibition. Certain things were indubitably Ordained. . . .

He arrived just after the official opening, on the first day. The rooms in which the exhibition was being held were crowded with aspiring and perspiring socialites, lured there either in the hope of collecting one of Mr. Vascoe's bacchanalian invitations to dinner, or because they hoped to be recognized by other socialites, or because they hoped to be mistaken for connoisseurs of Art, or just because they hadn't the courage to let anyone think that they couldn't spend five dollars on charity just as easily as anyone else. Simon Templar shouldered his way through them until he sighted Vascoe. He had done some thinking since he drove Meryl home, and it had only confirmed him in his conviction that Nemesis was due to overtake Mr. Vascoe at last. At the same time, Simon saw no reason why he shouldn't deal himself in on the party.

With Vascoe and Meryl was a tall and immaculately dressed young man with a pink face whose amiable stupidity was accentuated by a chin that began too late and a forehead that stopped too soon. Simon had no difficulty in identifying him as the Earl of Eastridge, and that was how Meryl introduced him before Vascoe turned round and recognized his unwelcome visitor.

"How did you get in here?" he brayed.

"Through the front door," said the Saint genially. "I put down my five bucks and they told me to walk right in. It's a public exhibition, I believe. Did you come in on a free pass?"

Vascoe recovered himself with difficulty but his large face remained an ugly purple.

"Come to have a look round, have you?" he asked offensively. "Well, you can look as much as you like. I flatter myself this place is burglarproof."

Meryl turned white, and the earl tittered. Other guests who were within earshot hovered expectantly—some of them, one might almost have thought, hopefully. But if they were waiting for a prompt and swift outbreak of violence, or even a sharp and candid repartee, they were doomed to disappointment. The Saint smiled with unruffled good humour.

Burglarproof, is it?" he said tolerantly. "You really think it's burglarproof. Well, well, *well!*" He patted Mr. Vascoe's bald head affectionately. "Now I'll tell you what I'll do, Fatty. I'll bet you twenty thousand dollars it's burgled within a week."

For a moment Vascoe seemed to be in a tangle with his own vocal cords. He could only stand and gasp like a fish.

"You—you have the effrontery to come here and tell me you're going to burgle my house?" he spluttered. "You—you ruffian! I'll have you handed over to the police! I never heard of such—such—such—"

"I haven't commited any crime yet, that I know of," said the Saint patiently. "I'm simply offering you a sporting bet. Of course, if you're frightened of losing . . ."

"Such God-damned insolence!" howled Vascoe furiously. "I've got detectives here—"

He looked wildly around for them.

"Or if twenty thousand dollars is too much for you," Simon continued imperturbably.

"I'll take your twenty thousand dollars," Vascoe retorted viciously. "If you've got that much money. I'd be glad to break you as well as see you sent to jail. And if anything happens after this, the police will know who to look for!"

"That will be quite a change for them," said the Saint. "And now, in the circumstances, I think we ought to have a stakeholder."

He scanned the circle of faces that had gathered round them and singled out a dark cadaverous-looking man who was absorbing the scene from the background with an air of disillusioned melancholy.

"I see Morgan Dean of the *Daily Mail* over there," he said. "Suppose we each give him our checks for twenty thousand dollars. He can pay them into his own bank, and write a check for forty thousand when the bet's settled. Then there won't be any difficulty about the winner collecting. What about it, Dean?"

The columnist rubbed his chin.

"Sure," he drawled lugubriously. "My bank'll probably die of shock, but I'll chance it."

"Then we're all set," said the Saint, taking out his checkbook. "Unless Mr. Vascoe wants to back out . . ."

Mr. Vascoe stared venomously from face to face. It was dawning on him that he was in a corner. If he had seen the faintest encouragement anywhere to laugh off the situation, he would have grabbed at the opportunity with both hands; but he looked for the encouragement in vain.He hadn't a single real friend in the room, and he was realist enough to know it. Already he could see heads being put together, could hear whispers. . . . He knew just what would be said if he backed down . . . and Morgan Dean would put the story on the front page . . .

Vascoe drew himself up and a malignant glitter came into his small eyes.

"It suits me," he said swaggeringly. "Mr. Dean will have my check this afternoon."

He stalked away, still fuming, and Morgan Dean's long sad face came closer to the Saint.

"Son," he said, "I like a good story as much as anyone. And I like you. And nobody'd cheer louder than me if Vascoe took a brodie. But don't you think you've bitten off more than you can chew? I know how much Vascoe loves you, and I'd say he'd almost be glad to spend twenty grand to see you in jail. Besides, it wouldn't do you any good. You couldn't sell stuff like this."

"You could sell it without the slightest trouble," Simon contradicted him. "There are any number of collectors who aren't particular how they make their collections and who don't care if they can show them to the public. And I've never been in jail, anyway—one ought to try everything once."

He spent the next hour going slowly round the exhibition, making careful written notes about the exhibits in his catalogue, while Vascoe watched him with his rage rising to the brink of apoplexy. He also examined all the windows and showcases, taking measurements and drawing diagrams with a darkly conspiratorial air, and only appearing to notice the existence of the two obvious detectives who followed him everywhere when he politely asked them not to breathe so heavily down his neck.

Fernack saw the headlines and nearly blew all the windows out of Centre Street. He burst into the Saint's apartment like a whirling dervish.

"What's the meaning of this?" he bugled brassily, thrusting a crumpled copy of the *Daily Mail* under the Saint's nose. "Come on—what is it?"

Simon looked at the quivering sheet.

" 'Film Star Says She Prefers Love,' " he read off it innocently. "Well, I suppose it means just that, Fernack. Some people are funny that way."

"I mean *this!*" blared the detective, dabbing at Morgan Dean's headline with a stubby forefinger. "I've warned you once, Templar; and, by God, if you try to win this bet I'll get you for it if it's the last thing I do!"

The Saint lighted a cigarette and leaned back.

"Aren't you being just a little bit hasty?" he inquired reasonably; but his blue eyes were twinkling with imps of mockery that sent cold shivers up and down the detective's spine. "All I've done is to bet that there'll be a burglary at Vascoe's within the week. It may be unusual, but is it criminal? If I were an insurance company—"

"You aren't an insurance company," Fernack said pungently. "But you wouldn't make a bet like that if you thought there was any risk of losing it."

"That's true. But that still doesn't make me a burglar. Maybe I was hoping to put the idea into somebody else's head. Now if you want to give your nastly suspicious mind something useful to work on, why don't you find out something about Vascoe's insurance?"

For a moment the audacity of the suggestion took Fernack's breath away. And then incredulity returned to his rescue.

"Yeah—and see if I can catch him burgling his own house so he can lose twenty thousand dollars!" He hooted. "Do you know what would happen if I let my suspicious mind have its own way? I'd have you arrested for vagrancy and keep you locked up for the rest of the week!"

The Saint nodded enthusiastically.

"Why don't you do that?" he suggested. "It'd give me a gorgeous alibi."

Fernack glared at him thoughtfully. The temptation to take the Saint at his word was almost overpowering. But the tantalizing twinkle in the Saint's eyes and the memory of many past encounters with the satanic guile of that debonair freebooter, filled Fernack's heated brain with a gnawing uneasiness that paralyzed him. The Saint must have considered that contingency: if Fernack carried out his threat, he might be doing the very thing that the Saint expected and wanted him to do—he might be walking straight into a baited trap that would elevate him to new pinnacles of ridiculousness before it turned him loose. The thought made him go hot and cold all over.

Which was exactly what Simon meant it to do.

"When I put you in the cooler," Fernack proclaimed loudly, "you're going to stay there for more than a week."

He stormed out of the apartment and went to interview Vascoe.

"With your permission, sir," he said, "I'd like to post enough men around this house to make it impossible for a mouse to get in."

Vascoe shook his head.

"I haven't asked for protection," he said coldly. "If you did that, the Saint would be forced to abandon the attempt. I should prefer him to make it. The Ingerbeck Agency is already employed to protect my collection. There are two armed guards in the house all day, and another man on duty all night. And the place is fitted with the latest burglar alarms. The only way it could be successfully robbed would be by an armed gang, and we know that the Saint doesn't work that way. No, Inspector. Let him get in. He won't find it so easy to get out again. And then I'll be very glad to send for you."

Fernack argued, but Vascoe was obstinate. He almost succeeded in convincing the detective of the soundness of his reasoning. There would be no triumph or glory in merely preventing the Saint from getting near the house, but to catch him red-handed would be something else again. Nevertheless, Fernack would have felt happier if he could have convinced himself that the Saint was possible to catch.

"At least, you'd better let me post one of my own men outside," he said.

"You will do nothing of the sort," Vascoe said curtly. "The Saint would recognize him a mile off. The police have had plenty of opportunities to catch him before this and I don't remember your making any brilliant use of them."

Fernack left the house in an even sourer temper than he had entered it, and if he had been a private individual he would have satisfied himself that anything that happened to Vascoe or his art treasures would be richly deserved. Unfortunately his duty didn't allow him to dispose of the matter so easily. He had another stormy interview with the Assistant Commissioner, who for the first time in history was sympathetic.

"You've done everything you could, Mr. Fernack," he said. "If Vascoe refuses to give us any assistance he can't expect much."

"The trouble is that if anything goes wrong, that won't stop him squawking," Fernack said gloomily.

Of all the persons concerned, Simon Templar was probably the most untroubled. For two days he peacefully followed the trivial rounds of his normal law-abiding life; and the plainclothes men whom Fernack had set to watch him, in spite of his instructions, grew bored with their vigil.

At about two o'clock in the morning of the third day his telephone rang.

"This is Miss Vascoe's chauffeur, sir," said the caller. "She couldn't reach a telephone herself so she asked me to speak to you. She said that she must see you."

Simon's blood ran a shade faster—he had been half expecting such a call.

"When and where?" he asked crisply.

"If you can be at the second traffic light going north in Central Park in an hour's time, sir—she'll get there as soon as she has a chance to slip away."

"Tell her I'll be there," said the Saint.

He hung up the instrument and looked out of the window. On the opposite pavement a man paced wearily up and down, as he had done for two nights before wondering why he should have been chosen for a job that kept him out of bed to so little purpose.

But on this particular night the monotony of the sleuth's existence was destined to be relieved. He followed his quarry on a brief walk which led to Fifty-second Street and into one of the many night haunts which crowd a certain section of that fevered thoroughfare, where the Saint was promptly ushered to a favoured table by a beaming head-waiter. The sleuth, being an unknown and unprofitable-looking stranger, was ungraciously hustled into an obscure corner. The Saint sipped a drink and watched the late floor show for a few minutes, and then got up and sauntered back through the darkened room towards the exit. The sleuth, noting with a practised eye that he had still left three quarters of his drink and a fresh packet of cigarettes on the table, and that he had neither asked for nor paid a check, made the obvious deduction and waited without anxiety for his return. After a quarter of an hour he began to have faint doubts of his wisdom, after half an hour he began to sweat, and in forty-five minutes he was in a panic. The lavatory attendant didn't remember noticing the Saint, and certainly he wasn't in sight when the detective arrived; the doorman was quite certain that he had gone out nearly an hour ago because he had left him two dollars to pay the waiter.

An angry and somewhat uncomfortable sleuth went back to the Saint's address and waited for some time in agony before the object of his attention came home. As soon as he was relieved at eight o'clock he telephoned headquarters to report the tragedy; but by then it was too late.

Inspector Fernack's eyes swept scorchingly over the company that had collected in Vascoe's drawing room. It consisted of Elliot Vascoe himself, Meryl, the Earl of Eastridge, an assortment of servants and the night guard from Ingerbeck's.

"I might have known what to expect," he complained savagely. "You wouldn't help me to prevent anything like this happening but after it's happened you expect me to clean up the mess. It'd serve you right if I told you to let your precious Ingerbeck do the cleaning up. If the Saint was here now—"

He broke off, with his jaw dropping and his eyes rounding into reddened buttons of half-unbelieving wrath.

The Saint was there. He was drifting through the door like a pirate entering a captured city, with an impotently protesting butler fluttering behind him like a flustered vulture—sauntering coolly in with a cigarette between his lips and blithe brows slanted banteringly over humorous blue eyes. He nodded to Meryl and smiled over the rest of the congregation.

"Hullo, souls," he murmured. "I heard I'd won my bet, so I toddled over to make sure."

For a moment Vascoe himself was gripped in the general petrifaction, and then he stepped forward, his face crimson with fury.

"There you are," he burst out incoherently. "You come here—you—There's your man, Inspector. Arrest him!"

Fernack's mouth clamped up again.

"You don't have to tell me," he said grimly.

"And just why," Simon inquired lazily, as the detective moved towards him, "am I supposed to be arrested?"

"Why?" screamed the millionaire. "You—you stand there and ask *why?* Because you've been too clever for once, Mr. Smarty. You said you were going to burgle this house, and you've done it—and now you're going to prison where you belong!"

The Saint leaned back against an armchair, ignoring the handcuffs that Fernack was dragging from his pocket.

"Those are harsh words, Comrade," he remarked reproachfully. "Very harsh. In fact, I'm not sure that they wouldn't be actionable. I must ask my lawyer. But would anybody mind telling me what makes you so sure that I did this job?"

"I'll tell you why." Fernack spoke. "Last night the guard got tired of working so hard and dozed off for a while." He shot a smoking glance at the wretched private detective who was trying to obliterate himself behind the larger members of the crowd. "When he woke up again, somebody had opened that window, cut the alarms, opened that centre showcase and taken about a hundred thousand dollars' worth of small stuff out of it. And that somebody couldn't resist leaving his signature." He jerked out a piece of Vascoe's own notepaper, on which had been drawn a spidery skeleton figure with an elliptical halo poised at a rakish angle over its round blank head. "You wouldn't recognize it, would you?" Fernack jeered sarcastically.

Even so, his voice was louder than it need have been. For, in spite of everything, at the back of his mind there was a horrible little doubt. The Saint had tricked him so many times, had led him up the garden path so often and then left him freezing in the snow, that he couldn't make himself believe that anything was certain. And that horrible doubt made his head swim as he saw the Saint's critical eyes rest on the drawing.

"Oh yes," said the Saint patiently. "I can see what it's meant to be. And now I suppose you'd like me to give an account of my movements last night."

"If you're thinking of putting over another of your patent alibis," Fernack said incandescently, "let me tell you before you start that I've already heard how you slipped the man I had watching you —just about the time that this job was done."

Simon nodded.

"You see," he said, "I had a phone message that Miss Vascoe wanted to see me very urgently and I was to meet her at the second traffic light going north in Central Park."

The girl gasped as everyone suddenly looked at her.

"But Simon—I didn't—"

Her hand flew to her mouth.

Fernack's eyes lighted with triumph as they swung back to the Saint.

"That's fine," he said exultantly. "And Miss Vascoe doesn't know anything about it. So who else is going to testify that you spent your time waiting there—the man in the moon?"

"No," said the Saint. "Because I didn't go there."

Fernack's eyes narrowed with the fog that was starting to creep into his brain.

"Well, what—"

"I was expecting some sort of call like that," said the Saint. "I knew somebody was going to knock off this exhibition—after the bet I'd made with Vascoe, the chance of getting away with it and having me to take the rap was too good to miss. I meant it to look good—that's why I made the bet. But of course our friend had to be sure I wouldn't have an alibi, and he was pretty cunning about it. He guessed that you'd be having me shadowed, but he knew that a message like he sent me would make me shake my shadow. And then I'd have a fine time trying to prove that I spent an hour or so standing under a traffic light in Central Park at that hour of the night. Only I'm pretty cunning myself, when I think about it, so I didn't go. I came here instead."

Fernack's mouth opened again.

"You—"

"What are we wasting *time* for?" snorted Vascoe. "He admits he was here—"

"I was here," said the Saint coolly. "You know how the back of the house goes practically down to the East River, and you have a little private garden there and a landing stage? I knew that if anything was happening, it'd happen on that side—it'd be too risky to do anything on the street frontage, where anybody might come by and see it. Well, things were happening. There was a man out there, but I beat him over the head and tied him up before he could make a noise. Then I waited around, and somebody opened the window from *inside* and threw out a parcel. So I picked it up and took it home. Here it is."

He took it out of his hip pocket—it was a very large parcel, and the bulge would have been easy to notice if anyone had got behind him.

Vascoe let out a hoarse yell, jumped at it and wrenched it out of his hands. He ripped it open with clawing fingers.

"My miniatures!" he sobbed. "My medallions— my cameos! My—"

"Here, wait a minute!"

Fernack thrust himself forward again, taking possession of the package. For a second or two the denouement had blown him sky-high, turned him upside down and left him with the feeling that the pit of his stomach had suddenly gone away on an unauthorized vacation; but now he had his bearings again. He faced the Saint with homicidal determination.

"It's a fine story," he said raspily. "But this is one time you're not going to get away with it. Yeah, I get the idea. You pull the job so you can win your bet and then you bring the stuff back with that fairy tale and think everything's going to be all right. Well, you're not going to get away with it! What happened to the guy you say you knocked out and tied up, and who else saw him, and who else saw all these things happen?"

The Saint smiled.

"I left him locked up in the garage," he said. "He's probably still there. As for who else saw him, Martin Ingerbeck was with me."

"Who?"

"Ingerbeck himself. The detective bloke. You see, I happened to help him with a job once, so I didn't see why I shouldn't help him with another.* So as soon as I guessed what was going to happen, I called him up and he met me at once and came along with me. He even recognized the bloke who opened the window, too."

"And who was that?" Fernack demanded derisively, but somehow his derision sounded hollow.

The Saint bowed.

"I'm afraid," he said, "it was the Earl of Eastridge."

His lordship stared at him pallidly.

"I think you must be mad," he said.

"It's preposterous!" spluttered Vascoe. "I happen to have made every inquiry about Lord Eastridge. There isn't the slightest doubt that he's—"

"Of course he is," said the Saint calmly. "But he wasn't always. It's a curious old English custom— a fellow can go around with one name for most of his life and then he inherits a title and changes his name without any legal formalities. It's funny that you should have been asking me about him, Fernack. His name used to be Dennis Umber. As soon as Meryl mentioned the Earl of Eastridge I remembered what it was that I'd read about him in the papers. I'd noticed that he came into an earldom when his uncle died. That's why I thought something like this might happen, and that's why I made that bet with Vascoe."

The night guard fizzed suddenly out of his retirement.

"That's right!" he exploded excitedly. "I'll bet it was him. I wondered why I went off to sleep like that. Well, about two o'clock *he* came downstairs

—said he was looking for something to read because he couldn't get to sleep—and got me to have a drink with him. It was just after he went upstairs again that I fell off. That drink must've been doped!''

Eastridge looked from side to side and his face twitched. He made a sudden grab at his pocket, but Fernack was too quick for him.

Simon Templar hitched himself off the armchair as the brief scuffle subsided.

"Well, that seems to be that," he observed languidly. "You'll have to wait for another chance, Fernack. Go home and take some lessons in detecting, and you may do better next time." He looked at Vascoe. "I'll see my lawyers later and find out what sort of a suit we can cook up on account of all the rude things you've been saying, but meanwhile I'll collect my check from Morgan Dean." Then he turned to Meryl. "I'm going to lend Bill Fulton the profits to pay off his debts with," he said. "I shall expect a small interest in his invention and a large slice of wedding cake.''

Before she could say anything he was gone. Thanks didn't interest him: he wanted breakfast.

* See *Saint Overboard,* a Charter Book.

VI   THE STAR PRODUCERS

MR. HOMER QUARTERSTONE was not, to be candid, a name to conjure with in the world of the Theater. It must be admitted that his experience behind the footlights was not entirely confined to that immortal line: "Dinner is served." As a matter of fact, he had once said "The Baron is here" and "Will there be anything further, madam?" in the same act; and in another never-to-be-forgotten drama which had run for eighteen performances on Broadway, he had taken part in the following classic dialogue:

> NICK: Were you here?
> JENKINS (*Mr. Homer Quarterstone*): No sir.
> NICK: Did you hear anything?
> JENKINS: No sir.
> NICK: A hell of a lot of use you are.
> JENKINS: Yes, sir.
>   (*Exit, carrying tray.*)

In the executive line, Mr. Quarterstone's career had been marked by the same magnanimous emphasis on service rather than personal glory. He had not actually produced any spectacles of resounding success but he had contributed his modest quota to their triumph by helping to carry chairs and tables on to the stage and arrange them according to the orders of the scenic director. And although he had not actually given his personal guidance to any of the financial manoeuvres associated with theatrical production, he had sat in the box office at more than one one-night stand, graciously controlling the passage over the counter of those fundamental monetary items without which the labours of more egotistical financiers would have been fruitless.

Nevertheless, while it is true that the name of Quarterstone had never appeared in any headlines, and that his funeral cortege would never have attracted any distinguished pallbearers, he had undoubtedly found the Theatre more profitable than many other men to whom it had given fame.

He was a man of florid complexion and majestic bearing, with a ripe convexity under his waistcoat and a forehead that arched glisteningly back to the scruff of his neck; and he had a taste for black homburgs and astrakhan-collared overcoats which gave an impression of great artistic prosperity. This prosperity was by no means illusory, for Mr. Homer Quarterstone, in his business capacity, was now the principal, president, director, owner and twenty-five percent of the staff of the Supremax Academy of Dramatic Art, which according to its frequent advertisements had been the training ground, the histrionic hothouse, so to speak, of many stars whose names were now household words from the igloos of Greenland to the tents of the wandering Bedouin. And the fact that Mr. Quarterstone had not become the principal, president, director, owner, etc., of the Supremax Academy until several years after the graduation of those illustrious personages, when in a period of unaccustomed affluence and unusually successful borrowing he had purchased the name and good will of an idealistic but moribund concern, neither deprived him of the legal right to make that claim in his advertising nor hampered the free flow of his imagination when he was expounding his own experience and abilities to prospective clients.

Simon Templar, who sooner or later made the acquaintance of practically everyone who was collecting too much money with too little reason, heard of him first from Rosalind Hale, who had been one of those clients; and she brought him her story for the same reason that many other people who had been foolish would often come to Simon Templar with their troubles, as if the words "The Saint" had some literally supernatural significance, instead of being merely the nickname with which he had once incongruously been christened.

"I thought it was only the sensible thing to do—to get some proper training—and his advertisements looked genuine. You wouldn't think those film stars would let him use their names for a fraud, would you? . . . I suppose I was a fool, but I'd played in some amateur things, and people who weren't trying to flatter me said I was good, and I really believed I'd got it in me, sort of instinctively. And *some* of the people who believe they've got it in them must be right, and they must do something about it, or else there wouldn't be any actors and actresses at all, would there? . . . And really I'm—I—well, I don't make you shudder when you look at me, do I?"

This at least was beyond argument, unless the looker was a crusted misogynist, which the Saint very firmly was not. She had an almost childishly heart-shaped face, with small features that were just far enough from perfection to be exciting, and her figure had just enough curves in just the right places.

The Saint smiled at her without any cynicism.

"And when you came into this money . . ."

"Well, it looked just like the chance I'd been dreaming about. But I still wanted to be intelligent about it and not go dashing off to Hollywood to turn into a waitress, or spend my time sitting in producers' waiting rooms hoping they'd notice me and just looking dumb when they asked if I had experience, or anything like that. That's why I went to Quarterstone. And he said I'd got everything, and I only wanted a little schooling. I paid him five hundred dollars for a course of lessons, and then another five hundred for an advanced course, and then another five hundred for a movie course and by that time he'd been talking to me so that he'd found out all about that legacy, and that was when his friend came in and they got me to give them four thousand dollars to put that play on."

"In which you were to play the lead."

"Yes, and—"

"The play never did go on."

She nodded, and the moistness of her eyes made them shine like jewels. She might not have been outstandingly intelligent, she might or might not have had any dramatic talent, but her own drama was real. She was crushed, frightened, dazed, wounded in the deep and desperate way that a child is hurt when it has innocently done something disastrous, as if she were still too stunned to realize what she had done.

Some men might have laughed, but the Saint didn't laugh. He said in his quiet friendly way: "I suppose you checked up on your legal position?"

"Yes. I went to see a lawyer. He said there wasn't anything I could do. They'd been too clever. I couldn't *prove* that I'd been swindled. There really was a play and it could have been put on, only the expenses ran away with all the money before that, and I hadn't got any more, and apparently that often happens, and you couldn't prove it was a fraud. I just hadn't read the contracts and things properly when I signed them, and Urlaub—that's Quarterstone's friend—was entitled to spend all that money, and even if he was careless and stupid you couldn't prove it was criminal. . . . I suppose it was my own fault and I've no right to cry about it but it was everything I had, and I'd given up my job as well, and—well, things have been pretty tough. You know."

He nodded, straightening a cigarette with his strong brown fingers.

All at once the consciousness of what she was doing now seemed to sweep over her, leaving her tongue-tied. She had to make an effort to get out the last words that everything else had inevitably been leading up to.

"I know I'm crazy and I've no right, but could you—could you think of anything to do about it?"

He went on looking at her thoughtfully for a moment, and then, incredulously, she suddenly realized that he was smiling, and that his smile was still without satire.

"I could try," he said.

He stood up, long immaculately tailored legs
gathering themselves with the lazy grace of a tiger,
and all at once she found something in his blue eyes
that made all the legends about him impossible to
question. It was as if he had lifted all the weight off
her shoulders without another word when he stood
up.

"One of the first things I should prescribe is a
man-sized lunch," he said. "A diet of doughnuts
and coffee never produced any great ideas."

When he left her it was still without any more
promises, and yet with a queer sense of certainty
that was more comforting than any number of
promises.

The Saint himself was not quite so certain; but
he was interested, which perhaps meant more. He
had that impetuously human outlook which judged
an adventure on the artistic quality rather than on
the quantity of boodle which it might contribute to
his unlawful income. He liked Rosalind Hale, and
he disliked such men as Mr. Homer Quarterstone
and Comrade Urlaub sounded as if they would be;
more than that, perhaps, he disliked rackets that
preyed on people to whom a loss of four thousand
dollars was utter tragedy. He set out that same afternoon to interview Mr. Quarterstone.

The Supremax Academy occupied the top floor
and one room on the street level of a sedate old-
fashioned building in the West Forties; but the entrance was so cunningly arranged and the other intervening tenants so modestly unheralded that any
impressionable visitor who presented himself first
at the ground-floor room labelled "Inquiries," and
who was thence whisked expertly into the elevator
and upwards to the rooms above, might easily have

been persuaded that the whole building was taken up with various departments of the Academy, a hive buzzing with ambitious Thespian bees. The brassy but once luscious blonde who presided in the Inquiry Office lent tone to this idea by saying that Mr. Quarterstone was busy, very busy, and that it was customary to make appointments with him days in advance; when she finally organized the interview it was with the regal generosity of a slightly flirtatious goddess performing a casual miracle for an especially favoured and deserving suitor—a beautifully polished routine that was calculated to impress prospective clients from the start with a gratifying sense of their own importance.

Simon Templar was always glad of a chance to enjoy his own importance, but on this occasion he regretfully had to admit that so much flattery was undeserved, for instead of his own name he had cautiously given the less notorious name of Tombs. This funereal anonymity, however, cast no shadow over the warmth of Mr. Quarterstone's welcome.

"My dear Mr. Tombs! Come in. Sit down. Have a cigarette."

Mr. Quarterstone grasped him with large warm hands, wrapped him up, transported him tenderly and installed him in an armchair like a collector enshrining a priceless piece of fragile glass. He fluttered anxiously round him, pressing a cigarette into the Saint's mouth and lighting it before he retired reluctantly to his own chair on the other side of the desk.

"And now, my dear Mr. Tombs," said Mr. Quarterstone at last, clasping his hands across his stomach, "how can I help you?"

Simon looked at his hands, his feet, the carpet, the wall and then at Mr. Quarterstone.

"Well," he said bashfully, "I wanted to inquire about some dramatic lessions."

"Some—ah—oh yes. You mean a little advanced coaching. A little polishing of technique?"

"Oh no," said the Saint hastily. "I mean, you know your business, of course, but I'm only a beginner."

Mr. Quarterstone sat up a little straighter and gazed at him.

"You're only a beginner?" he repeated incredulously.

"Yes."

"You mean to tell me you haven't any stage experience?"

"No. Only a couple of amateur shows."

"You're not joking?"

"Of course not."

"Well!"

"Mr. Quarterstone continued to stare at him as if he were something rare and strange. The Saint twisted his hatbrim uncomfortably. Mr. Quarterstone sat back again, shaking his head.

"That's the most extraordinary thing I ever heard of," he declared.

"But why?" Simon asked, with not unreasonable surprise.

"My dear fellow, anyone would take you for a professional actor! I've been in the theatrical business all my life—I was on Broadway for ten years, played before the King of England, produced hundreds of shows—and I'd have bet anyone I could pick out a professional actor every time. The way you walked in, the way you sat down, the way you use your hands, even the way you're smoking that cigarette—it's amazing! Are you *sure* you're not having a little joke?"

"Absolutely."

"May I ask what is your present job?"

"Until a couple of days ago," said the Saint ingenuously, "I was working in a bank. But I'd always wanted to be an actor, so when my uncle died and left me twenty thousand dollars I thought it was a good time to start. I think I could play parts like William Powell," he added, looking sophisticated.

Mr. Quarterstone beamed like a cat full of cream.

"Why not?" he demanded oratorically. "Why ever not? With that natural gift of yours . . ." He shook his head again, clicking his tongue in eloquent expression of his undiminished awe and admiration. "It's the most amazing thing! Of course, I sometimes see fellows who are nearly as good-looking as you are, but they haven't got your manner. Why, if you took a few lessons—"

Simon registered the exact amount of glowing satisfaction which he was supposed to register.

"That's what I came to you for, Mr. Quarterstone. I've seen your advertisements—"

"Yes, yes!"

Mr. Quarterstone got up and came round the desk again. He took the Saint's face in his large warm hands and turned it this way and that, studying it from various angles with increasing astonishment. He made the Saint stand up and studied him from a distance, screwing up one eye and holding up a finger in front of the other to compare his proportions. He stalked up to him again, patted him here and there and felt his muscles. He stepped back again and posed in an attitude of rapture.

"Marvellous!" he said "Astounding!"

Then, with an effort, he brought himself out of his trance.

"Mr. Tombs," he said firmly, "there's only one thing for me to do. I must take you in charge myself. I have a wonderful staff here, the finest staff you could find in any dramatic academy in the world, past masters, every one of 'em—but they're not good enough. I wouldn't dare to offer you anything but the best that we have here. I offer you myself. And because I only look upon it as a privilege—nay, a sacred duty, to develop this God-given talent you have, I shall not try to make any money out of you. I shall only make a small charge to cover the actual value of my time. Charles Laughton paid me five thousand dollars for one hour's coaching in a difficult scene. John Barrymore took me to Hollywood and paid me fifteen thousand dollars to criticize him in four rehearsals. But I shall only ask you for enough to cover my out-of-pocket expenses—let us say, one thousand dollars—for a course of ten special, personal, private, exclusive lessions. . . . No," boomed Mr. Quarterstone, waving one hand in a magnificent gesture, "don't thank me! Were I to refuse to give you the benefit of all my experience, I should regard myself as a traitor to my calling, a very—ah—Ishmael!"

If there was one kind of acting in which Simon Templar had graduated from a more exacting academy than was dreamed of in Mr. Quarterstone's philosophy, it was the art of depicting the virgin sucker yawning hungrily under the baited hook. His characterization was pointed with such wide-eyed and unsullied innocence, such eager and open-mouthed receptivity, such a succulently plastic amenability to suggestion, such a rich response to flattery—in a word, with such a sublime absorptiveness to the old oil—that men such as Mr. Quarterstone, on becoming conscious of him for the first time, had been known to wipe away a furtive tear as they dug down into their pockets for first mortgages on the Golden Gate Bridge and formulae for extracting radium from old toothpaste tubes. He used all of that technique on Mr. Homer Quarterstone, so effectively that his enrollment in the Supremax Academy proceeded with the effortless ease of a stratospherist returning to terra firma a short head in front of his punctured balloon. Mr. Quarterstone did not actually brush away an unbidden tear, but he did bring out an enormous leather-bound ledger and enter up particulars that Life, in spite of the pessimists, was not wholly without its moments of unshadowed joy.

"When can I start?" asked the Saint, when that had been done.

"Start?" repeated Mr. Quarterstone, savouring the word. "Why, whenever you like. Each lesson lasts a full hour, and you can divide them up as you wish. You can start now if you want to. I had an appointment . . ."

"Oh."

"But it is of no importance, compared with this." Mr. Quarterstone picked up the telephone. "Tell Mr. Urlaub I shall be too busy to see him this afternoon," he told it. He hung up. "The producer," he explained, as he settled back again. "Of course you've heard of him. But he can wait. One

day he'll be waiting on your doorstep, my boy.'' He
dismissed Mr. Urlaub, the producer, with a majestic *ademán*. "What shall we take first—eloqu-
tion?''

"You know best, Mr. Quarterstone," said the
Saint eagerly.

Mr. Quarterstone nodded. If there was anything
that could have increased his contentment, it was a
pupil who had no doubt that Mr. Quarterstone
knew best. He crossed his legs and hooked one
thumb in the armhole of his waistcoat.

"Say 'Eee.' "

"Eee."

"Ah."

Simon went on looking at him expectantly.

"Ah," repeated Mr. Quarterstone.

"I beg your pardon?"

"I said 'Ah.' "

"Oh."

"No, ah."

"Yes, I—"

"Say it after me, Mr. Tombs. '*Aaaah.*' Make it
ring out. Hold your diaphragm in, open your
mouth and bring it up from your chest. This is a
little exercise in the essential vowels."

"Oh. *Aaaah.*"

"Oh."

"Oh."

"I."

"I."

"*Ooooo.*"

"*Ooooo.*"

"Wrong."

"I'm sorry . . ."

"Say 'Wrong,' Mr. Tombs."

"Wrong."

"Right," said Mr. Quarterstone.

"Right."

"Yes, yes," said Mr. Quarterstone testily. "I—"

"Yes, yes, I."

Mr. Quarterstone swallowed.

"I don't mean you to repeat *every* word I say," he said. "Just the examples. Now let's try the vowels again in a sentence. Say this: 'Faaar skiiies loooom O-ver meee.'"

"Faaar skiiies loooom O-ver meee."

"Daaark niiight draaaws neeear."

"The days are drawing in," Simon admitted politely.

Mr. Quarterstone's smile became somewhat glassy, but whatever else he may have been he was no quitter.

"I'm afraid he is a fraud," Simon told Rosalind Hale when he saw her the next day. "But he has a beautiful line of sugar for the flies. I was the complete gawky goof, the perfect bank clerk with dramatic ambitions—you could just see me going home and leering at myself in the mirror and imagining myself making love to Greta Garbo—but he told me he just couldn't believe how anyone with my poise couldn't have had any experience."

The girl's white teeth showed on her lower lip.

"But that's just what he told me!"

"I could have guessed it, darling. And I don't suppose you were the first either. . . . I had two lessons on the spot, and I've had another two today; and if he can teach anyone anything worth knowing about acting, then I can train ducks to write shorthand. I was so dumb that anyone with an ounce of artistic feeling would have thrown me out of the window, but when I left him this afternoon he almost hugged me and told me he could hardly wait to finish the course before he rushed out to show me to Gilbert Miller."

She moved her head a little, gazing at him with big sober eyes.

"He was just the same with me, too. Oh, I've been such a fool!"

"We're all fools in our own way," said the Saint consolingly. "Boys like Homer are my job, so they don't bother me. On the other hand, you've no idea what a fool I can be with soft lights and sweet music. Come on to dinner and I'll show you."

"But now you've given Quarterstone a thousand dollars, and what are you going to do about it?"

"Wait for the next act of the stirring drama."

The next act was not long in developing. Simon had two more of Mr. Quarterstone's special, personal, private, exclusive lessons the next day, and two more the day after—Mr. Homer Quarterstone was no apostle of the old-fashioned idea of making haste slowly, and by getting in two lessons daily he was able to double his temporary income, which then chalked up at the very pleasing figure of two hundred dollars per diem, minus the overhead, of which the brassy blonde was not the smallest item. But this method of gingering up the flow of revenue also meant that its duration was reduced from ten days to five, and during a lull in the next day's first hour (Diction, Gesture and Facial Expression) he took the opportunity of pointing out that Success, while already certain, could never be too certain or too great, and therefore that a supplementary series of lessons in the Art and Technique of the Motion Picture, while involving only a brief delay, could only add to the magnitude of Mr. Tombs's ultimate inevitable triumph.

On this argument, for the first time, Mr. Tombs disagreed.

"I want to see for myself whether I've mastered the first lessons," he said. "If I could get a small part in a play, just to try myself out . . ."

He was distressingly obstinate, and Mr. Quarterstone, either because he convinced himself that it would only be a waste of time, or because another approach to his pupil's remaining nineteen thousand dollars seemed just as simple, finally yielded. He made an excuse to leave the studio for a few minutes, and Simon knew that the next development was on its way.

It arrived in the latter part of the hour (Declamation with Gestures, Movement and Facial Expression—The Complete Classical Scene).

Mr. Quartstone was demonstrating.

"To be," trumpeted Mr. Quarterstone, gazing ceilingwards with an ecstatic expression, the chest thrown out, the arms slightly spread, "or not to be." Mr. Quarterstone ceased to be. He slumped, the head bowed, the arms hanging listlessly by the sides, the expression doleful. "That—is the question." Mr. Quarterstone pondered it, shaking his head. The suspense was awful. He elaborated the idea. "Whether 'tis nobler"—Mr. Quarterstone drew himself nobly up, the chin lifted, the right arm turned slightly across the body, the forearm parallel with the ground—"in the mind"—he clutched his brow, where he kept his mind—"to suffer"—he clutched his heart, where he did his suffering—"the slings"—he stretched out his left hand for the slings—"and arrows"—he flung out

his right hand for the arrows—"of outrageous fortune"—Mr. Quarterstone rolled the insult
lusciously around his mouth and spat it out with
defiance—"or to take arms"—he drew himself up
again, the shoulders squared, rising slightly on tip-
toe—"against a sea of troubles"—his right hand
moved over a broad panorama, undulating sym-
bolically—"and by opposing"—the arms rising
slightly from the elbow, fists clenched, shoulders
thrown back, chin drawn in—"end them!"—the
forearms striking down again with a fierce chop-
ping movement, expressive of finality and knock-
ing a calendar off the table.

"Excuse me," said the brassy blonde, with
her head poking round the door. "Mr. Urlaub is
here."

"Tchah!" said Mr. Quarterstone, inspiration
wounded in mid-flight. "Tell him to wait."

"He said—"

Mr. Quarterstone's eyes dilated. His mouth
opened. His hands lifted a little from his sides, the
fingers tense and parted rather like plump claws,
the body rising. He was staring at the Saint.

"Wait!" he cried. "Of course! The very thing!
The very man you've got to meet! One of the
greatest producers in the world today! Your
chance!"

He leapt a short distance off the ground and
whirled on the blonde, his arm flung out, pointing
quiveringly.

"Send him in!"

Simon looked wildly breathless.

"But—but will he—"

"Of course he will! You've only got to remember
what I've taught you. And sit down. We must be
calm."

Mr. Quarterstone sank into a chair, agitatedly looking calm, as Urlaub bustled in. Urlaub trotted quickly across the room.

"Ah, Homer."

"My dear Waldemar! How is everything?"

"Terrible! I came to ask for your advice . . ."

Mr. Urlaub leaned across the desk. He was a smallish, thin, bouncy man with a big nose and sleek black hair. His suit fitted him as tightly as an extra skin, and the stones in his tiepin and in his rings looked enough like diamonds to look like diamonds. He moved as if he were hung on springs, and his voice was thin and spluttery like the exhaust of an anemic motorcycle.

"Niementhal has quit. Let me down at the last minute. He wanted to put some goddam gigolo into the lead. Some ham that his wife's got hold of. I said to him, 'Aaron, your wife is your business and this play is my business.' I said, 'I don't care if it hurts your wife's feelings and I don't care if she gets mad at you, I can't afford to risk my reputation on Broadway and my investment in this play by putting that ham in the lead.' I said, 'Buy her a box of candy or a diamond bracelet or anything or send her to Paris or something, but don't ask me to make her happy by putting that gigolo in this play.' So he quit. And me with everything set, and the rest of the cast ready to start rehearsing next week, and he quits. He said, 'All right, then use your own money.' I said, 'You know I've got fifty thousand dollars in this production already, and all you were going to put in is fifteen thousand, and for that you want me to risk my money and my reputation by hiring that ham. I thought you said you'd got a good actor.' 'Well, you find yourself a good actor and fifteen thousand dollars,' he says, and he quits.

Cold. And I can't raise another cent—you know how I just tied up half a million to save those aluminum shares."

"That's tough, Waldemar," said Mr. Quarterstone anxiously. "Waldemar, that's tough! . . . Ah —by the way—pardon me—may I introduce a student of mine? Mr. Tombs . . ."

Urlaub turned vaguely, apparently becoming aware of the Saint's presence for the first time. He started forward with a courteously extended hand as the Saint rose.

But their hands did not meet at once. Mr. Urlaub's approaching movement died slowly away, as if paralysis had gradually overtaken him, so that he finally came to rest just before they met, like a clockwork toy that had run down. His eyes became fixed, staring. His mouth opened.

Then, very slowly, he revived himself. He pushed his hand onwards again and grasped the Saint's as if it were something precious, shaking it slowly and earnestly.

"A pupil of yours, did you say, Homer?" he asked in an awestruck voice.

"That's right. My star pupil, in fact. I might almost say . . ."

Mr. Urlaub paid no attention to what Quarterstone might almost have said. With his eyes still staring, he darted suddenly closer, peered into the Saint's face, took hold of it, turned it from side to side, just as Quarterstone had once done. Then he stepped back and stared again, prowling round the Saint like a dog prowling round a tree. Then he stopped.

"Mr. Tombs," he said vibrantly, "will you walk over to the door, and then walk back towards me?"

Looking dazed, the Saint did so.

Mr. Urlaub looked at him and gulped. Then he hauled a wad of typescript out of an inside pocket, fumbled through it and thrust it out with one enamelled fingernail dabbing at a paragraph.

"Read that speech—read it as if you were acting it."

The Saint glanced over the paragraph, drew a deep breath and read with almost uncontrollable emotion.

"No, do not lie to me. You have already given me the answer for which I have been waiting. I am not ungrateful for what you once did for me, but I see now that that kind act was only a part of your scheme to ensnare my better nature in the toils of your unhallowed passions, as though pure love were a thing that could be bought like merchandise. Ah, yes, I loved you, but I did not know that that pretty face was only a mask for the corruption beneath. How you must have laughed at me! Ha, ha. I brought you a rose, but you turned it into a nest of vipers in my bosom. They have stabbed my heart! (Sobs.)"

"My God," he breathed hoarsely.

"What?" said the Saint.

"Why?" said Mr. Quarterstone.

"But it's like a miracle!" squeaked Waldemar Urlaub. "He's the man! The type! The face! The figure! The voice! The manner! He is a genius! Homer, where did you find him? The women will storm the theatre." He grasped the Saint by the arm, leaning as far as he could over the desk and over Mr. Quarterstone. "Listen. He must play that part. He must. He is the only man. I couldn't put anyone else in it now. Not after I've seen him. I'll

·show Aaron Niementhal where he gets off. Quit, did he? Okay. He'll be sorry. We'll have a hit that'll make history!"

"But Waldemar . . ."

Mr. Urlaub dried up. His clutching fingers uncoiled from Simon's arm. The fire died out of his eyes. He staggered blindly back and sank into a chair and buried his face in his hands.

"Yes," he whispered bitterly. "I'd forgotten. The play can't go on. I'm sunk, Homer—just for a miserable fifteen grand. And now, of all times, when I've just seen Mr. Tombs!"

"You know I'd help you if I could, Waldemar," said Mr. Quarterstone earnestly. "But I just bought my wife a fur coat, and she wants a new car, and that ranch we just bought in California set me back a hundred thousand."

Mr. Urlaub shook his head.

"I know. It's not your fault. But isn't it just the toughest break?"

Quarterstone shook his head in sympathy. And then he looked at the Saint.

It was quite a performance, that look. It started casually, beheld inspiration, blazed with triumph, winked, glared significantly, poured out encouragement, pleaded, commanded and asked and answered several questions, all in a few seconds. Mr. Quarterstone had not at any period in his career actually held down the job of prompter, but he more than made up with enthusiasm for any lack of experience. Only a man who had been blind from birth could have failed to grasp the idea that Mr. Quarterstone was suggesting, and the Saint had not strung along so far in order to feign blindness at the signal for his entrance.

Simon cleared his throat.

"Er—did you say you only needed another fifteen thousand dollars to put on this play?" he asked diffidently, but with a clearly audible note of suppressed excitement.

After that he had to work no harder than he would have had to work to get himself eaten by a pair of hungry lions. Waldemar Urlaub, once the great light had dawned on him, skittered about like a pea on a drum in an orgy of exultant planning. Mr. Tombs would have starred in the play anyhow, whenever the remainder of the necessary wind had been raised—Urlaub had already made up his mind to that—but if Mr. Tombs had fifteen thousand dollars as well as his genius and beauty, he would be more than a star. He could be co-producer as well, a sharer in the profits, a friend and an equal, in every way the heir to the position which the great Aaron Niementhal would have occupied. His name would go on the billing with double force—Urlaub grabbed a piece of paper and a pencil to illustrate it:

SEBASTIAN TOMBS
and
WALDEMAR URLAUB
present
SEBASTIAN TOMBS
in
"LOVE—THE REDEEMER"

There would also be lights on the theatre, advertisements, photographs, newspaper articles, news items, gossip paragraphs, parties, movie rights, screen tests, Hollywood, London, beautiful and adoring women . . . Mr. Urlaub built up a luminous picture of fame, success and fortune, while Mr. Quarterstone nodded benignly and slapped everybody on the back and beamed at the Saint at intervals with a sublimely smug expression of "I told you so."

"And they did all that to me, too," said Rosalind Hale wryly. "I was practically Sarah Bernhardt when they'd finished. . . . But I told you just how they did it. Why do you have to let yourself in for the same mess that I got into?"

"The easiest way to rob a bank is from the inside," said the Saint cryptically. "I suppose you noticed that they really have got a play?"

"Yes. I read part of it—the same as you did."

"Did you like it?"

She made a little grimace.

"You've got a right to laugh at me. I suppose that ought to have been warning enough, but Urlaub was so keen about it, and Quarterstone had already made me think he was a great producer, so I couldn't say that I thought it was awful. And then I wondered if it was just because I didn't know enough about plays."

"I don't know much about plays myself," said the Saint. "But the fact remains that Comrade Urlaub has got a complete play, with three acts and everything, god-awful though it is. I took it away with me to read it over and the more I look at it the more I'm thinking that something might be done with it."

Rosalind was aghast.

"You don't mean to say you'd really put your money into producing it?"

"Stranger things have happened," said the Saint thoughtfully. "How bad can a play be before it becomes good? And how much sense of humour is there in the movie business? Haven't you seen those reprints of old two-reelers that they show sometimes for a joke, and haven't you heard the audience laughing itself sick? . . . Listen. I only wish I knew who wrote *Love—the Redeemer*. I've got an idea . . ."

Mr. Homer Quarterstone could have answered his question for him, for the truth was that the author of *Love—the Redeemer* resided under the artistic black homburg of Mr. Homer Quarterstone. It was a matter of considerable grief to Mr. Quarterstone that no genuine producer had ever been induced to see eye to eye with him on the subject of the superlative merits of that amorous masterpiece, so that after he had grown weary of collecting rejections Mr. Quarterstone had been reduced to the practical expedient of using his magnum opus as one of the props in the more profitable but by no means less artistic drama from which he and Mr. Urlaub derived their precarious incomes; but his loyalty to the child of his brain had never been shaken.

It was therefore with a strange squirmy sensation in the pit of his stomach that Mr. Quarterstone sat in his office a few mornings later and gazed at a card in the bottom left-hand corner of which were the magic words, "*Paragon Pictures, Inc., Hollywood, Calif.*" A feeling of fate was about him, as if he had been unexpectedly reminded of a still-cherished childhood dream.

"Show her in," he said with husky magnificence.

The order was hardly necessary, for she came in at once, shepherded by a beaming Waldemar Urlaub.

"Just thought I'd give you a surprise, Homer," he explained boisterously. "Did your heart jump when you saw that card? Well, so did mine. Still, it's real. I fixed it all up. Sold her the play. 'You can't go wrong,' I said, 'with one of the greatest drammers ever written.' "

Mrs. Wohlbreit turned her back on him coldly and inspected Mr. Quarterstone. She looked nothing like the average man's conception of a female from Hollywood, being gaunt and masculine with a sallow lined face and gold-rimmed glasses and mousey hair plastered back above her ears, but Mr. Quarterstone had at least enough experience to know that women were used in Hollywood in executive positions which did not call for the decorative qualities of more publicized employees.

She said in her cold masculine voice: "Is this your agent?"

Mr. Quarterstone swallowed.

"Ah—"

"Part owner," said Mr. Urlaub eagerly. "That's right, isn't it, Homer? You know our agreement—fifty–fifty in everything. Eh? Well, I' been working on this deal—"

"I asked you," said Mrs. Wohlbreit penetratingly, "because I understand that you're the owner of this play we're interested in. There are so many chisellers in this business that we make it our policy to approach the author first direct—if he wants to take any ten-percenters in afterwards, that's his affair. A Mr. Tombs brought me the play first , and told me he had an interest in it. I found out that he got it from Mr. Urlaub, so I went to him. Mr. Urlaub told me that you were the original author. Now, who am I to talk business with?"

Mr. Quarterstone saw his partner's mouth opening for another contribution.

"With—with us," he said weakly.

It was not what he might have said if he had had time to think, but he was too excited to be particular.

"Very well," said Mrs. Wohbreit. "We've read this play, *Love—the Redeemer*, and we think it would make a grand picture. If you haven't done anything yet about the movie rights . . ."

Mr. Quarterstone drew himself up. He felt as if he was in a daze from which he might be rudely awakened at any moment, but it was a beautiful daze. His heart was thumping, but his brain was calm and clear. It was, after all, only the moment with which he had always known that his genius must ultimately be rewarded.

"Ah—yes," he said with resonant calm. "The movie rights are, for the moment, open to—ah—negotiation. Naturally, with a drama of such quality, dealing as it does with a problem so close to the lives of every member of the thinking public, and appealing to the deepest emotions and beliefs of every intelligent man and woman—"

"We thought it would make an excellent farce," said Mrs. Wohlbreit blandly. "It's just the thing we've been looking for for a long time." But before the stricken Mr. Quarterstone could protest, she had added consolingly: "We could afford to give you thirty thousand dollars for the rights."

"Ah—quite," said Mr. Quarterstone bravely.

By the time that Mrs. Wohlbreit had departed, after making an appointment for the contract to be signed and the check paid over at the Paragon offices the following afternoon, his wound had healed sufficiently to let him take Mr. Urlaub in his arms, as soon as the door closed, and embrace him fondly in an impromptu rumba.

"Didn't I always tell you that play was a knockout?" he crowed. "It's taken 'em years to see it, but they had to wake up in the end. Thirty thousand dollars! Why, with that money I can—" He sensed a certain stiffness in his dancing partner and hastily corrected himself: "I mean, we—we can—"

"Nuts," said Mr. Urlaub coarsely. He disengaged himself and straightened the creases out of his natty suit. "What you've got to do now is sit down and figure out a way to crowbar that guy Tombs out of this."

"Tombs?"

"Yeah! *He* wasn't so dumb. He had the sense to see that that play of yours was the funniest thing ever written. When we were talking about it in here he must have thought we thought it was funny, too."

Mr. Quarterstone was appalled as the idea of duplicity struck him.

"Waldemar—d'you think he was trying to—"

"No. I pumped the old battle-axe on the way here. He told her he only had a part interest, but he wanted to do something for the firm and give us a surprise—he thought he could play the lead in the picture, too."

"Has she told him—"

"Not yet. You heard what she said. She gets in touch with the author first. But we got to get him before he gets in touch with her. Don't you remember those contracts we signed yesterday? Fifty percent of the movie rights for him!"

Mr. Quarterstone sank feebly on to the desk.

"Fifteen thousand dollars!" He groaned. Then he brightened tentatively. "But it's all right,

Waldemar. He agreed to put fifteen thousand dollars into producing the play, so we just call it quits and we don't have to give him anything."

"You great fat lame-brained slob," yelped Mr. Urlaub affectionately. "Quits! Like hell it's quits! D'you think I'm not going to put that play on, after this? It took that old battle-axe to see it, but she's right. They'll be rolling in the aisles!" He struck a Quarterstoneish attitude. " *'I brought you a rose,'* " he uttered tremulously, " *'but you turned it into a nest of vipers in my bosom. They have stabbed my heart!'* My God! It's a natural! I'm going to put it on Broadway whatever we have to do to raise the dough—but we aren't going to cut that mug Tombs in on it."

Mr. Quarterstone winced.

"It's all signed up legal," he said dolefully. "We'll have to spend our own dough and buy him out."

"Get your hat," said Mr. Urlaub shortly. "We'll cook up a story on the way."

When Rosalind Hale walked into the Saint's apartment at the Waldorf-Astoria that afternoon, Simon Templar was counting crisp new hundred-dollar bills into neat piles.

"What have you been doing?" she said. "Burgling a bank?"

The Saint grinned.

"The geetus came out of a bank, anyway," he murmured. "But Comrades Quarterstone and Urlaub provided the checks. I just went out and cashed them."

"You mean they bought you out?"

"After a certain amount of haggling and squealing—yes. Apparently Aaron Niementhal changed his mind about backing the show, and Urlaub didn't want to offend him on account of Aaron offered to cut him in on another and bigger and better proposition at the same time; so they gave me ten thousand dollars to tear up the contracts, and the idea is that I ought to play the lead in Niementhal's bigger and better show."

She pulled off her hat and collapsed into a chair. She was no longer gaunt and masculine and forbidding, for she had changed out of a badly fitting tweed suit and removed her sallow make-up and thrown away the gold-rimmed glasses and fluffed out her hair again so that it curled in its usual soft brown waves around her face, so that her last resemblance to anyone by the name of Wohlbreit was gone.

"Ten thousand dollars," she said limply. "It doesn't seem possible. But it's real. I can see it."

"You can touch it, if you like," said the Saint. "Here." He pushed one of the stacks over the table towards her. "Fifteen hundred that you paid Quarterstone for tuition." He pushed another. "Four thousand that you put into the play." He drew a smaller sheaf towards himself. "One thousand that I paid for my lessons. Leaving three thousand five hundred drops of gravy to be split two ways."

He straightened the remaining pile, cut it in two and slid half of it on to join the share that was accumulating in front of her. She stared at the money helplessly for a second or two, reached out and touched it with the tips of her fingers, and then suddenly she came round the table and flung herself into his arms. Her cheek was wet where it touched his face.

"I don't know how to say it," she said shakily. "But you know what I mean."

"There's only one thing bothering me," said the Saint some time later, "and that's whether you're really entitled to take back those tuition fees. After all, Homer made you a good enough actress to fool himself. Maybe he was entitled to a percentage, in spite of everything."

His doubts, however, were set at rest several months afterwards, when he had travelled a long way from New York and many other things had happened, when one day an advertisement in a New York paper caught his eye:

14th Week! Sold out 3 months ahead!
The Farce Hit of the Season:
LOVE—THE REDEEMER
by HOMER QUARTERSTONE
Imperial Theatre
A Waldemar Urlaub Production

Simon Templar was not often at a loss for words, but on this occasion he was tongue-tied for a long time. And then, at last, he lay back and laughed helplessly.

"Oh, well," he said. "I guess they earned it."

VII   THE MAN WHO LIKED ANTS

"I WONDER what would have happened if you had gone into a respectable business, Saint," Ivar Nordsten remarked one afternoon.

Simon Templar smiled at him so innocently that for an instant his nickname might almost have seemed justified—if it had not been for the faint lazy twinkle of unsaintly mockery that stirred at the back of his blue eyes.

"The question is too farfetched, Ivar. You might as well speculate about what would have happened if I'd been a Martian or a horse."

They sat on the veranda of the house of Ivar Nordsten—whose name was not really Ivar Nordsten, but who was alive that day and the master of fabulous millions only because the course of one of the Saint's lawless escapades had once crossed his path at a time when death would have seemed a happy release. He of all living men should have had no wish to change the history of that twentieth-century Robin Hood, whose dark reckless face could be found photographed in half the police archives of the world, and whose gay impudence of outlawry had in its time set the underworlds of five continents buzzing like nests of infuriated wasps. But in that mood of idle fantasy which may well come with the after-lunch contentment of a warm Florida afternoon, Nordsten would have put forward almost any preposterous premise that might give him the pleasure of listening to his friend.

"It isn't as farfetched as that," he said. "You will never admit it, but you have many respectable instincts."

"But I have so many more disreputable ones to keep them under control," answered the Saint earnestly. "And it's always been so much more amusing to indulge the disreputable instincts. . . . No, Ivar, I mustn't let you make a paragon out of me. If I were quite cynically psychoanalyzing myself, I should probably say that the reason why I only soak the more obvious excrescences on the human race is because it makes everything okay with my respectable instincts and lets them go peacefully to sleep. Then I can turn all my disreputable impulses loose on the mechanical problem of soaking this obvious excrescence in some satisfying novel and juicy manner, and get all the fun of original sin out of it without any qualms of conscience."

"But you contradict yourself. The mere fact that you speak in terms of what you call 'an obvious excrescence on the human race' proves that you have some moral standards by which you judge him, and that you have some idealistic interest in the human race itself."

"The human race," said the Saint sombrely, "is a repulsive, dull, bloated, ill-conditioned and ill-favoured mass of dimly conscious meat, the chief justification for whose existence is that it provides a contrasting background against which my beauty and spiritual perfections can shine with a lustre only exceeded by your own."

"You have a natural modesty which I had never suspected," Nordsten observed gravely, and they both laughed. "But," he added, "I think you will get on well with Dr. Sardon."

"Who is he?"

"A neighbour of mine. We are dining with him tonight."

Simon frowned.

"I warned you that I was travelling without any dress clothes," he began, but Nordsten shook his head maliciously.

"Dr. Sardon likes dress clothes even less than you do. And you never warned me that you were coming here at all. So what could I do? I accepted his invitation a week ago, so when you arrived I could only tell Sardon what had happened. Of course he insisted that you must come with me. But I think he will interest you."

The Saint sighed resignedly and swished the highball gently around in his glass so that the ice clinked.

"Why should I be interested in any of your neighbours?" he protested. "I didn't come here to commit any crimes; and I'm sure all these people are as respectable as millionaires can be."

"Dr. Sardon is not a millionaire. He is a very brilliant biologist."

"What else makes him interesting?"

"He is very fond of ants," said Nordsten seriously, and the Saint sat up.

Then he finished his drink deliberately and put down the glass.

"Now I know that this climate doesn't agree

with you," he said. "Let's get changed and go down to the tennis court. I'll put you in your place before we start the evening."

Nevertheless he drove over to Dr. Sardon's house that evening in a mood of open-minded curiosity. Scientists he had known before, men who went down thousands of feet into the sea to look at globigerina ooze and men who devised complicated electrical gadgets in laboratories to manufacture gold; but this was the first time that he had heard of a biologist who was fond of ants. Everything that was out of the ordinary was prospective material for the Saint. It must be admitted that in simplifying his own career to elementary equations by which obvious excrescences on the human race could be soaked, he did himself less than justice.

But there was nothing about the square smoothshaven man who was introduced to him as Dr. Sardon to take away the breath of any hardened outlaw. He might perhaps have been an ordinary efficient doctor, possibly with an exclusive and sophisticated practice; more probably he could have been a successful stock-broker, or the manager of any profitable commercial business. He shook hands with them briskly and almost mechanically, seeming to summarize the Saint in one sweeping glance through his crisp-looking rimless pince-nez.

"No, you're not a bit late, Mr. Nordsten. As a matter of fact I was working until twenty minutes ago. If you had come earlier I should have been quite embarrassed."

He introduced his niece, a dark slender girl with a quiet and rather aloof beauty which would have been chilling if it had not been relieved by the friendly humour of her brown eyes. About her, Si-

mon admitted, there might certainly have been
things to attract the attention of a modern buccaneer.

"Carmen has been assisting me. She has a very
good degree from Columbia."

He made no other unprompted reference to his
researches, and Simon recognized him as the
modern type of scientist whose carefully cultivated
pose of matter-of-fact worldliness is just as fash-
ionable an affection as the mystical and bearded
eccentricity of his predecessors used to be. Dr.
Sardon talked about politics, about his golf handi-
cap and about the art of Otto Soglow. He was an
entertaining and effective conversationalist but he
might never have heard of such a thing as biology
until towards the close of dinner Ivar Nordsten
skillfully turned a discussion of gardening to the
subject of insect pests.

"Although, of course," he said, "you would not
call them that."

It was strange to see the dark glow that came
into Sardon's eyes.

"As a popular term," he said in his deep vibrant
voice, "I suppose it is too well established for me to
change it. But it would be much more reasonable
for the insects to talk about human pests."

He turned to Simon.

"I expect Mr. Nordsten has already warned you
about the—bee in my bonnet," he said; but he used
the phrase without smiling. "Do you by any chance
know anything about the subject?"

"I had a flea once," said the Saint reminiscently.
"I called him Goebbels. But he left me."

"Then you would be surprised to know how
many of the most sensational achievements of man
were surpassed by the insects hundreds of years

ago without any artificial aids." The finger tips of his strong nervous hands played a tattoo against each other. "You talk about the Age of Speed and Man's Conquest of the Air; and yet the fly *Cephenomia*, the swiftest living creature, can outpace the fastest of your boasted aeroplanes. What is the greatest scientific marvel of the century? Probably you would say radio. But Count Arco, the German radio expert, has proved the existence of a kind of wireless telegraphy, or telepathy, between certain species of beetle, which makes nothing of a separation of miles. Lakhovsky claims to have demonstrated that this is common to several other insects. When the *Redemanni* termites build their twenty-five-foot conical towers topped with ten-foot chimneys they are performing much greater marvels of engineering than building an Empire State Building. To match them, in proportion to our size, we should have to put up skyscrapers four thousand feet high—and do it without tools."

"I knew the ants would come into it," said Nordsten sotto voce.

Sardon turned on him with his hot piercing gaze.

"Termites are not true ants—the term 'white ants' is a misnomer. Actually they are related to the cockroach. I merely mentioned them as one of the most remarkable of the lower insects. They have a superb social organization, and they may even be superior strategists to the true ants, but they were never destined to conquer the globe. The reason is that they cannot stand light and they cannot tolerate temperatures below twenty degrees centigrade. Therefore, their fields of expansion are for ever limited. They are one of Nature's false beginnings. They are a much older species than man, and they

have evolved as far as they are likely to evolve. . . .
It is not the same with the true ants."

He leaned forward over the table, with his face
white and transfigured as if in a kind of trance.

"The true ant is the destined ruler of the earth.
Can you imagine a state of society in which there
was no idleness, no poverty, no unemployment, no
unrest? We humans would say that it was an unat-
tainable Utopia; and yet it was in existence among
the ants when man was a hairy savage scarcely dis-
tinguishable from an ape. You may say that it is
incompatible with progress—that it could only be
achieved in the same way that it is achieved by
domestic cattle. But the ant has the same instincts
which have made man the tyrant of creation in his
time. *Lasius fuliginosus* keeps and milks its own
domestic cattle, in the form of plant lice. *Polyergus
rufescens* and *Formica sanguinea* capture slaves and
put them to work. *Messor barbarus*, the harvesting
ant, collects and stores grain. The *Attini* cultivate
mushrooms in underground forcing houses. And
all these things are done, not for private gain, but
for the good of the whole community. Could man
in any of his advances ever boast of that?"

"But if ants have so many advantages," said the
Saint slowly, "and they've been civilized so much
longer than man, why haven't they conquered the
earth before this?"

"Because Nature cheated them. Having given
them so much, she made them wait for the last essential—pure physical bulk."   •

"The brontosaurus had enough of that," said
Nordsten, "and yet man took its place."

Sardon's thin lips curled.

"The difference in size between man and brontosaurus was nothing compared with the difference

in size between man and ant. There are limits to the
superiority of brain over brawn—even to the superiority of the brain of an ant, which in proportion
to its size is twice as large as the brain of a man.
But the time is coming . . ."

His voice sank almost to a whisper, and in the
dim light of candles on the table the smouldering
luminousness of his eyes seemed to leave the rest of
his face in deep shadow.

"With the ant, Nature overreached herself. The
ant was ready to take his place at the head of creation before creation was ready for him—before the
solar system had progressed far enough to give him
the conditions in which his body, and his brain
with it, his brain which in all its intrinsic qualities
is so much finer than the brain of man, could grow
to the brute size at which all its potentialities could
be developed. Nevertheless, when the solar system
is older, and the sun is red because the white heat
of its fire is exhausted, and the red light which will
accelerate the growth of all living cells is stronger,
the ant will be waiting for his turn. Unless Nature
finds a swifter instrument than Time to put right
her miscalculation . . ."

"Does it matter?" asked the Saint lightly, and
Sardon's face seemed to flame at him.

"It matters. That is only another thing which we
can learn from the ant—that individual profit and
ambition should count for nothing beside more en-
during good. Listen. When I was a boy I loved
small creatures. Among them I kept a colony of
ants. In a glass box. I watched them in their busy
lives, I studied them as they built their nest, I saw
how they divided their labour and how they lived
and died so that their common life could go on. I
loved them because they were so much better than

everyone else I knew. But the other boys could not understand. They thought I was soft and stupid. They were always tormenting me. One day they found my glass box where the ants lived. I fought them, but there were so many of them. They were big and cruel. They made a fire and they put my box on it, while they held me. I saw the ants running, fighting, struggling insanely—" The hushed voice tightened as he spoke until it became thin and shrill like a suppressed scream. "I saw them curling up and shriveling, writhing, tortured. I could hear the hiss of their seething agony in the flames. I saw them going mad, twisting—sprawling—blackening —*burning alive before my eyes*—"

"Uncle!"

The quiet voice of the girl Carmen cut softly across the muted shriek in which the last words were spoken, so quietly and normally that it was only in the contrast that Simon realized that Sardon had not really raised his voice.

The wild fire died slowly out of Sardon's eyes. For a moment his face remained set and frozen, and then, as if he had only been recalled from a fleeting lapse of attention, he seemed to come awake again with a slight start.

"Where was I?" he said calmly. "Oh yes. I was speaking about the intelligence of ants. . . . It is even a mistake to assume, because they make no audible sounds, that they have not just as excellent means of communication as ourselves. Whether they share the telepathic gifts of other insects is a disputed point but it is certain that in their antennae they possess an idiom which is adequate to all ordinary needs. By close study and observation it has even been possible for us to learn some of

the elementary gestures. The work of Karl
Escherich . . ."

He went into details, in the same detached in-
cisive tone in which he had been speaking before
his outburst.

Simon Templar's fingers stroked over the cloth,
found a crumb of bread and massaged it gradually
into a soft round pellet. He stole a casual glance at
the girl. Her aloof oval face was pale, but that
might have been its natural complexion; her com-
posure was unaltered. Sardon's outburst might
never have occurred, and she might never have had
to interrupt it. Only the Saint thought that he saw
a shadow of fear moving far down in her eyes.

Even after Carmen had left the table, and the
room was richening with the comfortable aromas
of coffee and liqueur, brandy and cigars, Sardon
was still riding his hobbyhorse. It went on for nearly an hour, until at one of the rare lulls in the discussion Nordsten said: "All the same, Doctor, you
are very mysterious about what this has to do with
your own experiments."

Sardon's hands rested on the table, white and
motionless, the fingers spread out.

"Because I was not ready. Even to my friends I
should not like to show anything incomplete. But
in the last few weeks I have disposed of my uncer-
tainty. Tonight, if you like, I could show you a little."

"We should be honoured."

The flat pressure of Sardon's hands on the table
increased as he pushed back his chair and stood up.

"My workshops are at the end of the garden," he
said, and blew out the four candles.

As they rose and followed him from the room,

Nordsten touched the Saint's arm and said in a low voice: "Are you sorry I dragged you out?"

"I don't know yet," answered the Saint soberly.

The girl Carmen rejoined them as they left the house. Simon found her walking beside him as they strolled through the warm moonlight. He dropped the remains of his cigar and offered his cigarette case; they stopped for a moment while he gave her a light. Neither of them spoke, but her arm slipped through his as they went on.

The blaze of lights which Sardon switched on in his laboratory wiped the dim silvery gloom out of their eyes in a crash of harsh glaring illumination. In contrast with the tasteful furnishings of the house, the cold white walls and bare tiled floor struck the Saint's sensitive vision with the hygienic and inhuman chill which such places always gave him. But Sardon's laboratory was not like any other place of that kind in which he had ever been.

Ranged along the walls were rows of big glass-fronted boxes, in which apparently formless heaps of litter and rubble could be dimly made out. His eye was caught by a movement in one of the boxes, and he stepped up to look at it more closely. Almost in the same moment he stopped, and nearly recoiled from it, as he realized that he was looking at the largest ant that he had ever seen. It was fully six inches long; and, magnified in that proportion, he could see every joint in its shiny armour-plated surface and the curious bifurcated claws at the ends of its legs. It stood there with its antennae waving gently, watching him with its bulging beady eyes . . .

"*Tetramorium cespitum*," said Dr. Sardon, standing beside him. "One of my early experiments. Its natural size is about three tenths of an inch, but it did not respond very well to treatment."

"I should say it had responded heroically," said the Saint. "You don't mean you can do better than that?"

Sardon smiled.

"It was one of my early experiments," he repeated. "I was then merely trying to improve on the work of Ludwig and Ries of Berne, who were breeding giant insects almost comparable with that one, many years ago, with the aid of red light. Subsequently I discovered another principle of growth which they had overlooked, and I also found that an artificial selective cross-breeding between different species not only improved the potential size but also increased the intelligence. For instance, here is one of my later results—a combination of *Oecophylla smaragdina* and *Prenolepis imparis*."

He went to one of the longer and larger boxes at the end of the room. At first Simon could see nothing but a great mound of twigs and leaves piled high in one corner. There were two or three bones, stripped bare and white, lying on the sandy floor of the box. . . . Then Sardon tapped on the glass, and Simon saw with a sudden thrill of horror that what had been a dark hole in the mound of leaves was no longer black and empty. There was a head peering out of the shadow—dark bronze-green, iridescent, covered with short sparse bristly hairs. . . .

"*Oecophylla* is, of course, one of the more advanced species," Sardon was saying, in his calm precise manner. "It is the only known creature other than man to use a tool. The larvae secrete a substance similar to silk, with which the ants weave leaves together to make their nests, holding the larvae in their jaws and using them as shuttles. I don't yet know whether my hybrid has inherited that instinct."

"It looks as if it would make a charming pet, anyway," murmured the Saint thoughtfully. "Sort of improved lap dog, isn't it?"

The faint sly smile stayed fixed on Sardon's thin lips. He took two steps further, to a wide sliding door that took up most of the wall at the end of the laboratory, and looked back at them sidelong.

"Perhaps you would like to see the future ruler of the world," he said, so very softly that it seemed as if everyone else stopped breathing while he spoke.

Simon heard the girl beside him catch her breath, and Nordsten said quickly: "Surely we've troubled you enough already—"

"I should like to see it," said the Saint quietly.

Sardon's tongue slid once over his lips. He put his hand up and moved a couple of levers on the glittering panels of dials and switches beside the door. It was to the Saint that his gaze returned, with that rapt expression of strangely cunning and yet childish happiness.

"You will see it from where you stand. I will ask you to keep perfectly still, so as not to draw attention to yourselves—there is a strain of *Dorylina* in this one. *Dorylina* is one of the most intelligent and highly disciplined species, but it is also the most savage. I do not wish it to become angry—"

His arms stretched out to the handle of the door. He slid it aside in one movement, standing with his back to it, facing them.

The girl's cold hand touched the Saint's wrist. Her fingers slipped down over his hand and locked in with his own, clutching them in a sudden convulsive grip. He heard Ivar Nordsten's suppressed gasp as it caught in his throat, and an icy tingle ran up his spine and broke out in a clammy dew on his forehead.

The rich red light from the chamber beyond the door spilled out like liquid fire, so fierce and vivid that it seemed as if it could only be accompanied by the scorching heat of an open furnace; but it held only a slight appreciable warmth. It beat down from huge crimson arcs ranged along the cornices of the inner room among a maze of shining tubes and twisted wires; there was a great glass ball opposite in which a pale yellow streak of lightning forked and flickered with a faint humming sound. The light struck scarlet highlights from the gleaming bars of a great metal cage like a gigantic chicken coop which filled the centre of the room to within a yard of the walls. And within the cage something monstrous and incredible stood motionless, staring at them.

Simon would see it sometimes, years afterwards, in uneasy dreams. Something immense and frightful, glistening like burnished copper, balanced on angled legs like bars of plated metal. Only for a few seconds he saw it then, and for most of that time he was held fascinated by its eyes, understanding something that he would never have believed before. . . .

And then suddenly the thing moved, swiftly and horribly and without sound; and Sardon slammed the door shut, blotting out the eye-aching sea of red light and leaving only the austere cold whiteness of the laboratory.

"They are not all like lap dogs," Sardon said in a kind of whisper.

Simon took out a handkerchief and passed it across his brow. The last thing about that weird scene that fixed itself consciously in his memory was the girl's fingers relaxing their tense grip on his hand, and Sardon's eyes, bland and efficient and businesslike again, pinned steadily on them both in a sort of secret sneer. . . .

"What do you think of our friend?" Ivar Nordsten asked, as they drove home two hours later.

Simon stretched out a long arm for the lighter at the side of the car.

"He is a lunatic—but of course you knew that. I'm only wondering whether he is quite harmless."

"You ought to sympathize with his contempt for the human race."

The red glow of the Saint's cigarette end brightened so that for an instant the interior of the car was filled with something like a pale reflection of the unearthly crimson luminance which they had seen in Dr. Sardon's forcing room.

"Did you sympathize with his affection for his pets?"

"Those great ants?" Nordsten shivered involuntarily. "No. That last one—it was the most frightful thing I have ever seen. I suppose it was really alive?"

"It was alive," said the Saint steadily. "That's why I'm wondering whether Dr. Sardon is harmless. I don't know what you were looking at, Ivar, but, I'll tell you what made my blood run cold. It wasn't the mere size of the thing—though any common or garden ant would be terrifying enough if you enlarged it to those dimensions. It was worse than that. It was the proof that Sardon was right. That ant was looking at me. Not like any other insect or even animal that I've ever seen, but like an insect with a man's brain might look. That was the most frightening thing to me. *It knew!*"

Nordsten stared at him.

"You mean that you believe what he was saying about it being the future ruler of the world?"

"By itself, no," answered Simon. "But if it were not by itself—"

He did not finish the sentence; and they were silent for the rest of the drive. Before they went to bed he asked one more question.

"Who else knows about these experiments?"

"No one, I believe. He told me the other day that he was not prepared to say anything about them until he would show complete success. As a matter of fact, I lent him some money to go on with his work, and that is the only reason he took me into his confidence. I was surprised when he showed us his laboratory tonight—even I had never seen it before."

"So he is convinced now that he can show a complete success," said the Saint quietly, and was still subdued and preoccupied the next morning.

In the afternoon he refused to swim or play tennis. He sat hunched up in a chair on the veranda, scowling into space and smoking innumerable cigarettes, except when he rose to pace restlessly up and down like a big nervous cat.

"What you are really worried about is the girl," Nordsten teased him.

"She's pretty enough to worry about," said the Saint shamelessly. "I think I'll go over and ask her for a cocktail."

Nordsten smiled.

"If it will make you a human being again, by all means do," he said. "If you don't come back to dinner I shall know that she is appreciating your anxiety. In any case, I shall probably be very late myself. I have to attend a committee meeting at the golf club and that always adjourns to the bar and goes on for hours."

But the brief tropical twilight had already given way to the dark before Simon made good his threat. He took out Ivar Nordsten's spare Rolls-Royce and drove slowly over the highway until he found the turning that led through the deep cypress groves to the doctor's house. He was prepared to feel foolish; and yet as his headlights circled through the iron gates he touched his hip pocket to reassure himself that if the need arose he might still feel wise.

The trees arching over the drive formed a ghostly tunnel down which the Rolls chased its own fore-rush of light. The smooth hiss of the engine accentuated rather than broke the silence, so that the mind even of a hardened and unimaginative man might cling to the comfort of that faint sound in the same way that the mind of a child might cling to the light of a candle as a comfort against the gathering terrors of the night. The Saint's lips curled cynically at the flight of his own thoughts. . . .

And then, as the car turned a bend in the drive, he saw the girl, and trod fiercely on the brakes.

The tires shrieked on the macadam and the engine stalled as the big car rocked to a standstill. It flashed through the Saint's mind at that instant, when all sound was abruptly wiped out, that the stillness which he had imagined before was too complete for accident. He felt the skin creep over his back, and had to call on an effort of will to force himself to open the door and get out of the car.

She lay face downwards, halfway across the

drive, in the pool of illumination shed by the glaring headlights. Simon turned her over and raised her head on his arm. Her eyelids twitched as he did so; a kind of moan broke from her lips, and she fought away from him, in a dreadful wildness of panic, for the brief moment before her eyes opened and she recognized him.

"My dear," he said, "what has been happening?"

She had gone limp in his arms, the breath jerking pitifully through her lips, but she had not fainted again. And behind him, in that surround of stifling stillness, he heard quite clearly the rustle of something brushing stealthily over the grass beside the drive. He saw her eyes turning over his shoulder, saw the wide horror in them.

"*Look!*"

He spun round, whipping the gun from his pocket, and for more than a second he was paralyzed. For that eternity he saw the thing; deep in the far shadows, dimly illuminated by the marginal reflections from the beam of the headlights—something gross and swollen, a dirty grey-white, shaped rather like a great bleached sausage, hideously bloated. Then the darkness swallowed it again, even as his shot smashed the silence into a hundred tiny echoes.

The girl was struggling to her feet. He snatched at her wrist.

"This way."

He got her into the car and slammed the door. Steel and glass closed round them to give an absurd relief, the weak unreasoning comfort to the naked flesh which men under a bombardment find in cowering behind canvas screens. She slumped against his shoulder, sobbing hysterically.

"Oh, my God. My God!"

"What was it?" he asked.

"It's escaped again. I knew it would. He can't handle it—"

"Has it got loose before?"

"Yes. Once."

He tapped a cigarette on his thumbnail, stroked his lighter. His face was a beaten mask of bronze and granite in the red glow as he drew the smoke down into the mainspring of his leaping nerves.

"I never dreamed it had come to that," he said. "Even last night, I wouldn't have believed it."

"He wouldn't have shown you that. Even when he was boasting, he wouldn't have shown you. That was his secret . . . And I've helped him. Oh God," she said. "I can't go on!"

He gripped her shoulders.

"Carmen," he said quietly. "You must go away from here."

"He'd kill me."

"You must go away."

The headlamps threw back enough light for him to see her face, tear-streaked and desperate.

"He's mad," she said. "He must be. Those horrible things can't go on. Something terrible is going to happen. One day I saw it catch a dog . . . Oh, my God, if you hadn't come when you did —"

"Carmen." He still held her, speaking slowly and deliberately, putting every gift of sanity that he possessed into the level dominance of his voice. "You must not talk like this. You're safe now. Take hold of yourself."

She nodded.

"I know. I'm sorry. I'll be all right. But—"

"Can you drive?"

"Yes."

He started the engine and turned the car round. Then he pushed the gear lever into neutral and set the hand brake.

"Drive this car," he said. "Take it down to the gates and wait for me there. You'll be close to the highway, and there'll be plenty of other cars passing for company. Even if you do see anything, you needn't be frightened. Treat the car like a tank and run it over. Ivar won't mind—he's got plenty more. And if you hear anything, don't worry. Give me half an hour, and if I'm not back go to Ivar's and talk to him."

Her mouth opened incredulously.

"You're not getting out again?"

"I am. And I'm scared stiff." The ghost of a smile touched his lips, and then she saw that his face was stern and cold. "But I must talk to your uncle."

He gripped her arm for a moment, kissed her lightly and got out. Without a backward glance he walked quickly away from the car, up the drive towards the house. A flashlight in his left hand lanced the darkness ahead of him with its powerful beam, and he swung it from left to right as he walked, holding his gun in his right hand. His ears strained into the gloom which his eyes could not penetrate, probing the silence under the soft scuff of his own footsteps for any sound that would give him warning; but he forced himself not to look back. The palms of his hands were moist.

The house loomed up in front of him. He turned off to one side of the building, following the direction in which he remembered that Dr. Sardon's laboratory lay. Almost at once he saw the squares of lighted windows through the trees. A dull clang of sound came to him, followed by a sort of furious thumping. He checked himself; and then as he walked on more quickly some of the lighted windows went black. The door of the laboratory opened as the last light went out, and his torch framed Dr. Sardon in the doorway in its yellow circle.

Sardon was pale and dishevelled, his clothes awry. One of his sleeves was torn, and there was a scratch on his face from which blood ran. He flinched from the light as if it had burned him.

"Who is that?" he shouted.

"This is Simon Templar," said the Saint in a commonplace tone. "I just dropped in to say hullo."

Sardon turned the switch down again and went back into the laboratory. The Saint followed him.

"You just dropped in, eh? Of course. Good. Why not? Did you run into Carmen, by any chance?"

"I nearly ran over her," said the Saint evenly.

The doctor's wandering glance snapped to his face. Sardon's hands were shaking, and a tiny muscle at the side of his mouth twitched spasmodically.

"Of course," he said vacantly. "Is she all right?

"She is quite safe." Simon had put away his gun before the other saw it. He laid a hand gently on the other's shoulder. "You've had trouble here," he said.

"She lost her nerve," Sardon retorted furiously. "She ran away. It was the worst thing she could do. They understand, these creatures. They are too much for me to control now. They disobey me. My commands must seem so stupid to their wonderful brains. If it had not been that this one is heavy and waiting for her time—"

He checked himself.

"I knew," said the Saint calmly.

The doctor peered up at him out of the corners of his eyes.

"You knew?" he repeated cunningly.

"Yes. I saw it."

"Just now?"

Simon nodded.

"You didn't tell us last night," he said. "But it's what I was afraid of. I have been thinking about it all day."

"You've been thinking, have you? That's funny." Sardon chuckled shrilly. "Well, you're quite right. I've done it. I've succeeded. I don't have to work any more. They can look after themselves now. That's funny, isn't it?"

"So it is true. I hoped I was wrong."

Sardon edged closer to him.

"You hoped you were wrong? You fool! But I would expect it of you. You are the egotistical human being who believes in his ridiculous conceit that the whole history of the world from its own birth, all the species and races that have come into being and been discarded, everything—everything has existed only to lead up to his own magnificent presence on the earth. Bah! Do you imagine that your miserable little life can stand in the way of the march of evolution? Your day is over! Finished! In there"—his arm stiffened and pointed—"in there you can find the matriarch of the new ruling race of the earth. At any moment she will begin to lay her eggs, thousands upon thousands of them, from which her sons and daughters will breed—as big as she is, with her power and her brains." His voice dropped. "To me it is only wonderful that I should have been Nature's chosen instrument to give them their rightful place a million years before Time would have opened the door to them."

The flame in his eyes sank down as his voice sank and his features seemed to relax so that his square clean-cut efficient face became soft and beguiling like the face of an idiot child.

"I know what it feels like to be God," he breathed.

Simon held both his arms.

"Dr. Sardon," he said, "you must not go on with this experiment."

The other's face twisted.

"The experiment is finished," he snarled. "Are you still blind? Look—I will show you."

He was broad-shouldered and powerfully built, and his strength was that of a maniac. He threw off the Saint's hand with a convulsive wrench of his body and ran to the sliding door at the end of the room. He turned with his back to it, grasping the handle, as the Saint started after him.

"You shall meet them yourself," he said hoarsely. "They are not in their cage any more. I will let them out here, and you shall see whether you can stand against them. Stay where you are!"

A revolver flashed in his hand; and the Saint stopped four paces from him.

"For your own sake, Dr. Sardon," he said, "stand away from that door."

The doctor leered at him crookedly.

"You would like to burn my ants," he whispered.

He turned and fumbled with the spring catch, his revolver swinging carelessly wide from its aim; and the door had started to move when Simon shot him twice through the heart.

Simon was stretched out on the veranda, sipping

a highball and sniping mosquitoes with a cigarette end, when Nordsten came up the steps from his car. The Saint looked up with a smile.

"My dear fellow," said Nordsten, "I thought you would be at the fire."

"Is there a fire?" Simon asked innocently.

"Didn't you know? Sardon's whole laboratory has gone up in flames. I heard about it at the club, and when I left I drove back that way thinking I should meet you. Sardon and his niece were not there, either. It will be a terrible shock for him when he hears of it. The place was absolutely gutted—I've never seen such a blaze. It might have been soaked in gasoline. It was still too hot to go near, but I suppose all his work has been destroyed. Did you miss Carmen?"

The Saint pointed over his shoulder.

"At the present moment she's sleeping in your best guest room," he said. "I gave her enough of your sleeping tablets to keep her like that till breakfast time."

Nordsten looked at him.

"And where is Sardon?" he asked at length.

"He is in his laboratory."

Nordsten poured himself out a drink and sat down.

"Tell me," he said.

Simon told him the story. When he had finished, Nordsten was silent for a while. Then he said: "It's all right, of course. A fire like that must have destroyed all the evidence. It could all have been an accident. But what about the girl?"

"I told her that her uncle had locked the door and refused to let me in. Her evidence will be enough to show that Sardon was not in his right mind."

"Would you have done it anyhow, Simon?"

The Saint nodded.

"I think so. That's what I was worried about, ever since last night. It came to me at once that if any of these brutes could breed—" He shrugged a little wearily. "And when I saw that great queen ant, I knew that it had gone too far. I don't know quite how rapidly ants can breed, but I should imagine that they do it by thousands. If the thousands were all the same size as Sardon's specimens, with the same intelligence, who knows what might have been the end of it?"

"But I thought you disliked the human race," said Nordsten.

Simon got up and strolled across the veranda.

"Taken in the mass," he said soberly, "it will probably go on nauseating me. But it isn't my job to alter it. If Sardon was right, Nature will find her own remedy. But the world has millions of years left, and I think evolution can afford to wait."

His cigarette spun over the rail and vanished into the dark like a firefly as the butler came out to announce dinner; and they went into the dining room together.

WATCH FOR THE SIGN OF THE SAINT!

HE WILL BE BACK!

Page-turning Suspense from
CHARTER BOOKS